Also by A. J. Paquette

Nowhere Girl

Rules for Ghosting

Rules for Ghosting

A. J. Paquette

WALKER BOOKS FOR YOUNG READERS
AN IMPRINT OF BLOOMSBURY
NEW YORK   LONDON   NEW DELHI   SYDNEY

First published in the United States of America in July 2013
by Walker Books for Young Readers, an imprint of Bloomsbury Publishing, Inc.
www.bloomsbury.com

For information about permission to reproduce selections from this book, write to
Permissions, Walker BFYR, 1385 Broadway, New York, New York 10018
Bloomsbury books may be purchased for business or promotional use. For information on
bulk purchases, please contact Macmillan Corporate and Premium Sales Department
at specialmarkets@macmillan.com

Library of Congress Cataloging-in-Publication Data
Paquette, Ammi-Joan.
Rules for ghosting / A.J. Paquette.
p.   cm.
Summary: Joined by a living boy whose family has recently moved into the house she haunts,
Dahlia, a twelve-year-old ghost, tries to solve the mystery of her own death while fending off
an unscrupulous ghosthunter.
ISBN 978-0-8027-3454-9 (hardcover) · ISBN 978-0-8027-3455-6 (ebook)
[1. Ghosts—Fiction. 2. Haunted houses—Fiction. 3. Friendship—Fiction.] I. Title.
PZ7.P2119Ru 2013   [Fic]—dc23   2012027332

Book design by Nicole Gastonguay
Typeset by Westchester Book Composition
Printed and bound in the U.S.A. by Thomson-Shore Inc., Dexter, Michigan
2 4 6 8 10 9 7 5 3 1

All papers used by Bloomsbury Publishing, Inc., are natural, recyclable products
made from wood grown in well-managed forests. The manufacturing processes
conform to the environmental regulations of the country of origin.

For Zack: for everything

Rules for Ghosting

Chapter 1

Dahlia was dead, but the sunflower was not. Not yet, anyway. It still looked shimmery and only half-visible, just like all other living things. But the stem was bent and broken, and drooped down from the rest of the plant. Soon it would expire—right into Dahlia's waiting hands. Then she would carry the new ghost flower to her garden.

Feeling tingly all the way to the tips of her fingers, Dahlia studied her garden. It wasn't much—two spiky marigolds, a handful of daisies, and a stunted sprig of lavender—but it had taken her weeks to get right: finding and collecting the ghost flowers; jamming the expired stems deep into the ground and arranging them just so; making sure they didn't gust away in the stubborn October winds. Not easy, that was for sure. Why did everything dead always want to *rise*?

But the sunflower was something special. She'd waited a long time for a flower this perfect. Of course, time was something she had plenty of. For years and years she'd been a ghost, first keeping an eye on old Mrs. Silverton— her mother, Dahlia knew, but the crotchety old lady was so far from the smiling mama she remembered that she almost thought of her as a separate person—and then, after Mrs. Silverton had left, ghosting the manor all on her lonesome.

And what *about* that distant past, when Dahlia was alive? She remembered being very young. She remembered *that* Mrs. Silverton, her own mama, with the curling bob and the smiling eyes—and her father too, tall and stern. She remembered birthday cake and tooth fairy treats and learning to ride a bicycle. And then ... nothing. After her tenth birthday, it was like a patch was stuck over her brain. She didn't even remember how she had died.

Still, there was nothing Dahlia could do about all that— and today was sunflower day. She rolled onto her stomach, her nose inches from the plant. She curled her hand just outside the stem.

Any

    second

       now.

But no. The flower still hung forlornly in place.

Dahlia sighed. As she did, her ghost breath swirled around the flower, and slowly, so slowly, the live sunflower broke off and fell to the ground. In the same instant, a clear, sharp image pulled away from the dying flower and started to float away. Finally! Dahlia reached for it.

She had it, right at the tips of her fingers, but then she heard something. A sound—wait—a *voice*?

"Hello-o!" came the call again. "Tut-tut in there! Anybody ho-ome?"

Dahlia froze. A person! A real live person approaching Silverton Manor! Still—this sunflower was awfully perfect. And she'd been stalking it for ages. The person could go ahead and do what people did and Dahlia would investigate further in a minute.

Then a gust of wind took the choice—and the sunflower— right out of her hands. The expired flower bobbed end over end, heading away from Dahlia's grasp, heading toward the voice, but also—also—

—toward the Boundary.

No!

Dahlia somersaulted in place for momentum and shot through the air, pushing off on the heel of the wind-wave. She rocketed after the sunflower.

Dahlia was fast. The flower was faster. Just ahead was the tall wrought-iron gate that marked the edge of the Silverton Manor grounds. The Boundary. The arriving person marched toward the gate. Dahlia kept her focus on the flower. She sprang into a dive.

It was a gamble, and the second her body hit the airflow,

Dahlia knew she wouldn't make it. She didn't care; she had to at least try. She pushed everything she had after the sunflower, willing her arms to be longer, her legs stronger, just enough so she could—

The sunflower slipped through the gate.

SMACK! Barely a moment too late, Dahlia crashed into the Boundary. She hit it with a crunch that jarred her molecules and turned the world around her into scrambled eggs. Though Dahlia suspected it was she and not the world that was temporarily coming apart.

She hung there, suspended, for a full second, then slid down the Boundary and hovered in a mushy heap above the ground. Dahlia lifted her head. One of the marigolds had come loose from her garden patch and now bobbed right next to her nose—not laughing at her, exactly, but definitely looking smug.

Stupid ghost flower.

With a sniff, Dahlia rolled over and shimmied off the ground. She gave herself a good shake and patted her body up and down, making sure every part of her was in the right place. Hitting the Boundary never seemed to hurt her permanently, but it would take her hours to feel completely right after such a jolt. This time, it felt like something *in* her had broken loose a little too.

It wasn't even that losing the flower mattered so much, though she had wanted it badly. But every time she tried to pass the Boundary and failed, Dahlia felt something inside her sink further, some knot in her chest twist a little tighter, a small voice in her head whisper, *You will never leave this place. And you'll always, always be alone.*

"Hello-o . . ."

Dahlia jumped. The voice! It was closer now—just outside the gate. Well, at least she'd have something to distract her from her gloomy thoughts.

The early morning sun was in her eyes, but Dahlia squinted through the bars of the gate, which looked just as fuzzy and half-erased as everything in the living world did to her. Up the gravel path walked a small, pointy woman. She was shaped like an upside-down exclamation mark, and seemed nearly as excitable. A green flannel coat enveloped a long flowery dress, and on the woman's head rode a wide-brimmed hat topped with a cluster of bluebells. Dahlia thought how great those flowers would look in her garden. What was left of her garden.

"Yoo-hoo over there!" The woman was very near now, both hands lifted above her head in an animated wave. In another minute, the wrought iron bars wavered. She marched through them and beamed at Dahlia. "Well, I have arrived, and there's a mercy. Quite a fine secluded spot you have here!"

Dahlia's mouth opened. She hung motionless. "Wait—" she said. "Did you just . . ." Then something occurred to her. "Would you please say something else?"

"Excuse me?"

There it was again. That voice. It was so crystal clear that every sound Dahlia had heard before suddenly seemed dull and faint, like a TV show with the sound way down. And when she angled her body a little she could see it right away too, what she'd missed being so distracted with the sunflower. Unlike the smudgy-looking gate, the bushes, the trees, the house—all of which belonged to the living world—the new arrival looked vivid and bright and sharply outlined. And she had walked *through* the gate, of course.

"You're a ghost, aren't you?" Dahlia cried. "And you really are talking to *me*?"

"Why, yes indeed I am, dearie!" The woman paused. "Haven't you ever met another ghost?"

Dahlia shook her head. She'd occasionally seen other ghosts in the distance, had even called out to them a few times. But she'd never actually gotten one's attention. And now— what could she say? Another ghost! Really and truly, after all this time! Dahlia half wanted to burst out in a joyful little dance, but she decided against it.

The woman's face was a road map of fine lines, but her eyes were bright. With a twinkle and a nod, she linked an arm through Dahlia's. "How do you do, my dear? My name is Tibbs—Mrs. Libby Tibbs, that is. But you may call me Mrs. Tibbs."

Dahlia grinned. After long years of one-way conversations, it was such a strange sensation to be spoken *to* that she almost couldn't find the words to answer.

"The name reminds me of my dear husband, you see. Ah,

but that's a story for another day! And you are Dahlia Silverton, correct?"

"Yes, that's me!" Once the words started coming, they erupted in one long rush. "Oh—I just—can't believe you're *really* a ghost! I'm so used to everything around me looking all faint and foggy all the time. But you . . . you look like my expired things. You're *real*."

Mrs. Tibbs's laugh clanged like a rusty cowbell. "That I am! Oh, that I am. Well now, how about you show me around? But gracious!" She dropped Dahlia's arm and slapped her own forehead. "I do believe I left my bag out there somewhere. I set it down while trying to get your attention earlier." Without pausing, she bobbed off toward the gate.

"No, wait!" Dahlia yelled. But then—

The woman stepped easily through the gate, just as she had earlier, and returned two seconds later hefting a red paisley carpetbag.

Dahlia's jaw dropped. "But you—but it—the Boundary . . ." Frowning, she scooted over. Maybe the new ghost's arrival had dislodged it at last? Dahlia inched toward the gate, aware that Mrs. Tibbs was watching her curiously. She reached out her hand, pushed it toward the bars, and gave a sudden thrust.

The Boundary was as solid as ever. Her hand crumpled on itself, and Dahlia felt her eyes swim with sudden tears. She brushed them away quickly and slid back toward Mrs. Tibbs. "Never mind," she whispered.

Not a ghost-proof Boundary after all. Just a Dahlia-proof one.

She started heading back toward the manor house, but then she heard Mrs. Tibbs's voice behind her: "It's not you who's the problem, dear."

Dahlia slowly turned. "What did you say?"

"You can't leave the property, I expect?"

"I call it the Boundary," Dahlia said. "It's always been like this. I can move anywhere I want inside the house, all over the grounds—but never outside the gate. It's . . . not me, you say? Truly?"

"Certainly not, my dear." Mrs. Tibbs sighed. "You've always been alone here, haven't you?"

"I've pretty much been the only ghost. A few crickets hung around with me for a few days, and once a newborn kitten stayed so long I thought we might be pals for good. But," Dahlia said, studying the buckle on her shoes, trying not to think about the bubble of emptiness that had surrounded her for so long, "eventually it always ended up being just me. And my . . . mother, of course, when she was still here. But she went away about fifteen years ago."

"Ah, your mother. Ernestine Silverton?"

"That's right! But how did you . . ."

Mrs. Tibbs tapped the side of her hat. "There's a great deal more than you'd suspect lurking up here, my ghost-child. But all good things in their proper order. I can see there's much you need to learn and," she harrumphed, "quite providentially,

I've been sent to kick off this whole grand adventure. What do you say we go somewhere more comfortable, get settled in a bit, and then I can start you right at the beginning?"

Dahlia took a deep breath. Just having a visitor was a novelty in itself, not to mention having someone to talk to and hearing everything this newcomer had to say. With a growing smile, she spun back to face the house. "Let's go," she said. "I've got just the place. Comfortable, quiet, and perfectly ghostly. I have a feeling this is going to be quite the adventure!"

Chapter 2

Oliver Day got his first glimpse of their new house from a distance. They'd driven through two whole states trying to arrive before dark yesterday, but then they'd stopped for food a couple miles away in Longbrook and his parents got to talking with the locals, and that was the end of that. By the time they'd finished, it was ink-black outside, and everyone insisted that Silverton Manor must not be first approached in the dark of night—or at all, if possible, but that seemed unavoidable given the Day family's new position.

The villagers explained in low whispers that the manor house was cursed, and Mom and Dad dismissed that as utterly ridiculous. But the shudders and terrified looks were persuasive enough that they decided to stay overnight in the cobwebby Longbrook Inn. This morning they had enjoyed a greasy home-cooked breakfast, firmly taken their leave, and now here they were at last, winding up the forested road that led to the manor.

Their new home! The thought gave Oliver a little thrill, curse or no curse, even though he knew perfectly well that it wasn't *their* home—they were only house sitters, after all—and they would only be there for the next six months. Still, no matter how often they moved, Oliver couldn't help secretly hoping each time that this new house would end up being *the one*. The one they stayed in and never had to leave.

"There!" His ten-year-old sister Poppy was leaning so far out her window that both of the twins had to grab her belt loops to keep her from falling out. Still, she clearly had the best view, and Oliver put down his well-thumbed copy of *The Hound of the Baskervilles* to look where she was pointing. "Pull over, Daddy!" Poppy called.

"Shouldn't we keep driving? We'll see it better if we actually, you know, get there first . . . ," Mom said doubtfully. But by now Dad had pulled up on the bank and Poppy had her door half-open. If there ever was a chance to be first, fastest, or best at anything, Poppy could always be counted on to take it.

In a matter of seconds they had all piled out behind Poppy onto the dewy stretch of grass. The trees grew up densely around them, overhanging the road, which wound off into the distance like a timid earthworm. From there it swept up and away, ending in a gentle rump of a hill. And crowning the very top of that hill were the cranberry walls and shingled rooftops of Silverton Manor.

"Wow!" breathed Joe, even though at age six he was probably too young to really get what was going on. In fact, Oliver wasn't sure either Joe or Junie was fully awake. Oliver tended to think of the twins as a single two-headed, four-legged creature, since they were never apart from each other—and were usually up to some mischief. They even had a special Bag of Pranks they liked to lug around, though thankfully it was safely stowed in the trunk. Oliver called them JJ. Now he realized that JJ was actually facing the wrong direction, looking back down the road the way they'd come.

Oliver turned, and frowned. "Dad—" he said, and the rest of the family moved to follow his gaze. There was a car approaching, a very shiny car that seemed to make its own light, curving around the bend toward them like another sun rising. For a second it looked like it would sail right on past, but at the very last moment the driver swerved off the road, pulled up behind their road-weary minivan, and slid out of the front seat, all in one smooth oily motion.

"Mr. and Mrs. Day, I presume?" called the new arrival. He wore chunky mirrored sunglasses over a handlebar mustache, and his teeth were so white that Oliver had to squint a little.

"Jock Rutabartle, Longbrook Town commissioner, at your service."

"Er," said Mr. Day, clearing his throat. "Yes, of course. A pleasure to meet you in person at last."

Rutabartle's outstretched hand was like a motorized shaking machine, making its way around the circle from one person to the next, almost like it was independent from his body. Then he clasped his hands behind his back and gazed off toward the manor. "There she is," he said with a reverent sigh. "You'll want to get a closer look at her, I'm sure. Heading that way now, I suppose? And beginning to think about getting settled in, of course. A lovely family—most ordinary and pleasant-looking. Yes, isn't that so! Well—perhaps we should be moving along?"

Oliver had no idea what to make of this new guy, except that he was obviously a bit of a weirdo. But he appeared to be in charge, so . . .

"Yes. I suppose we should," Dad agreed.

Rutabartle reached up and fiddled with the edge of his glasses, then tugged on his mustache. "I know you collected the keys and information packet already from the office, but I figured I would come in person and give you an extra-hearty welcome. Introduce you to the manor and all that." With another clap of his hands, Rutabartle pivoted in place. He swung open his car door and was inside in a flash.

With one hand on the ignition, he stretched an arm out of his open window. "Both in my capacity as your landlord, and as a personal friend of the late Mrs. Silverton, who passed away so tragically these few weeks ago"—he dabbed the corner of each eye behind his dark lenses—"it is my honor to help you settle into your new position, to introduce you to your new . . . home . . . and to share some information which will assist you in this transition. Some very *significant* information." He waggled his eyebrows meaningfully. "Shall we?"

Without waiting for an answer, Rutabartle revved his

engine, skidded onto the road, and was gone so fast that Oliver half-expected to see his mustache still quivering in the air behind him.

As Mom and Dad moved toward the minivan, looking faintly puzzled, Oliver piled into the back after Poppy and JJ, and they set their course to the manor house. But somehow, the early morning sunshine didn't seem nearly as cheerful as it had a few minutes ago. Oliver wondered if it was the fall breeze chilling the air, or if that was a cold shiver of premonition tiptoeing up and down his spine.

Chapter 3

The house has been empty for years, ever since Mrs. Silverton left for the nursing home," Dahlia said, gesturing grandly as they melted through the heavy oak doorframe into the foyer. "Though there were some guys with clipboards swarming all over the place last week. And now you! It's all rather thrilling. Something in the air, do you suppose?"

"Ah," said Mrs. Tibbs. "Timing, yes, as to that—"

"Don't mind that broken window. Some vandals tried to get in this summer, as they will keep trying to do. This is a popular place for dares, what with all the rumors going around. Let's see." She counted on her fingers. "There's supposed to be a curse going back a hundred years or more, though I've no idea why anyone would think that, and of course the place is thought to be haunted. Obviously, one of those stories is true and the other is total bunk." She giggled and swished farther into the house. "I'm not especially good at haunting, as hard as

I've tried, but I can usually whip up enough of a ghostwhirl to send any snoopy rascals packing."

"Dahlia, my dear—"

"Mostly I stick to the lower floors. The upper ones are so easy to fall through . . . but I'm sure you know all about that. Those living objects, always turning to mush when you want to put your full weight on them!"

Dahlia zipped through the dust-covered dining room, across another room that was piled high with sheet-draped furniture, then glanced over her shoulder at Mrs. Tibbs as she neared her destination.

"Now, child, I really think we need to . . ."

Mrs. Tibbs's words trailed off, and no wonder! They'd come to Dahlia's favorite place in the whole house: her cozy add-on, nestled just off the sunroom and made of 100 percent expired goods. "What do you think?" she asked, puffing out her chest. "It's my own little ghost cubby."

Mrs. Tibbs moved through the outer wall of the manor into the ghostly addition. "But how? Where did this come from?"

It was a relief to slip out of the fuzzy-looking house and onto her ghost-solid floor. The room was a neat half circle, tacked on to the sunroom like an afterthought. A soft, worn armchair filled one end and the pale morning sun chased tiny polka-dot leaf shadows around a plush indigo floor throw. "I know it's small, but it's wonderful, isn't it? Mrs. Silverton started building the room decades ago—got it mostly done, in fact, but it was horribly damaged in a freak storm and she had

it torn down. It expired right in front of me, so I grabbed it
and kept it for my own. A lot of work, that was, but so worth
it! I patched it up, obviously, and added things over the years . . ."
She trailed off at the expression on Mrs. Tibbs's face; it looked
like a giant question mark had gotten lodged in her throat.
"What? Did I say something wrong?"

"Expired?" said Mrs. Tibbs faintly, shifting in place and
tucking her carpetbag closer to her side.

"Well, yes—you know, ghost stuff! That's how I get all my
treasures. When something goes in the bonfire, or it gets broken beyond repair, anything like that. If I'm right there when
it expires, I can catch its ghost essence and keep it. Isn't that
what everyone does?"

Mrs. Tibbs opened her mouth as though to answer, then
shook her head. "This room is lovely, my dear, but the manor
house is huge! It must have more than a dozen rooms. You
could live in any one of them."

"I know. But it's so hard, isn't it?" She waved her hand
toward the sunroom, with its fuzzy-outlined couches and half-
erased-looking end tables. "I can't relax in a room that's see-
through. I'm always falling through beds or slipping into chair
seats by mistake. Sometimes I *almost* think I can make contact, but it never quite works."

Mrs. Tibbs raised an eyebrow.

Dahlia flopped into the armchair. "I got this piece in the
last burglary a couple of months ago. Some hoodlums got ahold
of it and used it for target practice, I'm sorry to say." She looked

down, shame-faced. "I was on the other side of the property, ah, stargazing. By the time I caught on, they'd caused all sorts of trouble. This chair was so badly damaged that it expired with just a sneeze. But it's perfect for sleeping in."

"Sleeping?" Mrs. Tibbs asked.

These little clipped sentences were starting to make Dahlia nervous. As if to emphasize this, Mrs. Tibbs leaned over and put her hand on Dahlia's arm. "Dahlia, dear, if you don't mind my asking—you've been here for years now, right?"

Dahlia nodded.

"Well—what do you . . . *do* all day long?"

Dahlia stared. "What do I *do*? Why, there's so much! I spend a lot of time scouting for new objects, waiting for ones that are about to expire. I garden, when I can. I . . ." She blushed a little. "I like the stars and I spend a lot of time on that. Watching them and, er, taking notes. Sometimes I take naps during the day. Oh, I know I don't have to sleep—it's just the sunshine gets so warm and lulling through these windows. And I practice my haunting techniques. That's quite a lot, don't you think?" Yet her voice trailed off a little by the end. The more she recounted what she knew, the more she was starting to suspect that she might know very little after all. Maybe she should stop talking so much and focus on getting some answers.

"Mrs. Tibbs," she said, jumping up and grabbing the older ghost's hands. "I've been so excited to have you here, listening, that I haven't let you get a word in edgewise. Who are you, really? Why are you here? Does it have anything to do with me?"

"My most gracious ghostling," exclaimed Mrs. Tibbs. "I thought you would never ask! Who am I? Why, I'm a Liberator, of course—and I'm here to Liberate you."

"Liberate me?" Dahlia swallowed a sudden stutter. "You mean—do you mean to help get me past the Boundary?"

Mrs. Tibbs bobbed her head. "That and more! Oh, that and more."

This was even better than Dahlia had dared hope. She dropped her voice to a whisper. "So . . . you'll—get me out of here? Truly? Can we sail away—right now?"

"Ah, my dear." Mrs. Tibbs lowered her eyes. "If you could leave, you'd have gone long ago, wouldn't you? But you haven't gone, and that's why I'm here. I spoke before about Ernestine Silverton. Well, your mother crossed over to the Other Side nineteen days ago. And the very first thing she did after completing orientation was request a visitation with her daughter."

"Her daughter?"

"Her daughter, Dahlia Silverton, who was supposed to have crossed over fifty-eight years previously."

Dahlia felt faint. "But—I didn't cross over! I'm still here."

"Yes, quite. That would be the sweet smack of bureaucracy you're hearing. One of the wonders of modern ghost life, but land's sakes, the red tape it brings along with it."

"I don't . . ."

Mrs. Tibbs sighed. "You fell through the cracks, my dear. I'm sorry to say it but that's a fact. Crossover normally happens automatically, but when something goes wrong, a Liberator is supposed to show up on the double. *Within a Day of Death*, that's the official slogan. But . . . the truth is that sometimes the necessary forms get mislaid. Or lost altogether. Cases like this are sadly not at all uncommon."

"So this happens a lot then?" Dahlia wasn't sure if that made her feel better or worse. "But how can you help me now? After all these years . . ."

Mrs. Tibbs rubbed her hands together gleefully. "Ah, now we come to the heart of the matter. I am a Liberator, and it's my job to help free ghosts who are stuck. That's what I do! That is to say, *you* are my assignment. Why can't you leave this property, you ask? It's because you're Anchored."

"Anchored?"

"Yes—something from your past has hold of you and isn't letting go. Most unfortunately therefore, we cannot just fly away right now. But soon enough—yes, soon enough we'll have you busting out of here. I'm Mrs. Libby Tibbs, and I'm here to see you Liberated, right and proper. Now, where's my Pin?"

Mrs. Tibbs leaned up and probed around the side of her hat. With a grin and a wink, she extracted from the side a thick shiny hairpin that was longer than her hand. She grabbed the other end, pulled the two sides apart, and the pin opened wide into a shimmering high-tech scroll. "Personal Intelligence Nub—*Pin*—what do you think of that? Now, let me check in."

She waved a hand over the top of the glowing screen. "Silverton Manor, 1 Manor Drive, Longbrook?"

Dahlia nodded.

"Good. Now if you could supply your print here." Mrs. Tibbs slid the Pin over. There were lines and lines of text, and a spot marked PRINT. Dahlia sank her palm into the center. It closed around her fingers like a handful of soapsuds, then after a moment gave a refined ding. Dahlia pulled her hand off.

Mrs. Tibbs took the Pin back. She paged through a few screens, her fingers moving at lightning speed. "Thank you. Now, date and manner of death? Just for the record, you understand."

Dahlia scuffed at the rug with the sole of her patent-leather shoe. Was it weird that she had no idea when or how she had died? What would Mrs. Tibbs think?

"Ah," said the Liberator. "We'll leave that blank, I'm guessing. Don't be alarmed, my dear—it's not at all unusual."

"Will that make it harder to . . . to Liberate me?"

"Well, it certainly does add a level of challenge. But luckily, to me, challenge is nothing more than a great bundle of fun in disguise." Her eyes twinkled. "Never you fear, my good little gadfly. We'll crack this house open in no time and dig out its mysteries like walnut meat."

In spite of her uncertainty, Dahlia grinned. She had never thought of Silverton Manor as a walnut, nor as being very mysterious. But now that she thought about it, being stuck here all alone, not being able to leave for years and years, just wasn't normal. And now she knew something else too: Mrs. Silverton—no, *her mother*—was looking for her.

For as long as she could remember, Dahlia had tried to shut herself off from any emotion relating to her mother. It was easier that way, living as they did in their separate dimensions, unable to interact between the ghost and the living worlds. And she'd never had any sense that she was on her mother's mind, or that her mother missed her at all.

But now, this! Her mother had crossed over to the other side—had *died,* that was what it came down to—and one of the very first things she'd done was ask after *Dahlia*! All those years in silence, had her mother been missing Dahlia just as much as Dahlia had missed her?

A lump rose in Dahlia's throat, even as her emotions crystallized into a hard core of determination. Whatever it took, she *would* delve into her past, figure out what there was to know, and then find a way to leave Silverton Manor.

And then she would find a way to cross over once and for all.

Chapter 4

The old iron gate looked like it had come straight out of one of Oliver's creepy gothic novels. The bars were topped with ancient rusted curlicues, and the two heavily padlocked sides came together in an elaborate letter S. It was exactly the kind of place that would be expected to have its own curse. By the time Jock Rutabartle got the gate open and they all drove through, Oliver was hopping up and down in his seat with excitement.

Up close, the cranberry paint was obviously peeling, and the turrets and spires didn't gleam so much as glower. But to Oliver it was a dream house: at least three stories high, maybe four if those were attic windows peeking out of the very tip-top. This was a house that could outlast a hundred games of hide-and-seek and still feel brand new; a house that had its own face and its own brain, and probably talked to you in your sleep; a house of spooky mystery and mayhem and charm.

The cars ground down the gravel driveway and skirted the edges of the forest on their left, passing wide neglected fields—like the ghosts of ancient lawns and flowerbeds—on the right.

Oliver had a strange feeling in his middle—a feeling like hot chocolate with extra marshmallows, like the first big pool splash of summer . . . a feeling like coming home. He turned toward his parents in the front seat. Did they feel it too?

Dad was peering out the front window from under the brim of his lucky hat, his mouth curved sharply downward. His face looked like an hourglass with the sand slowly draining out. "I . . . ," Dad mumbled, swallowing. "Perhaps I should have come to see it before signing all the paperwork." He glanced at Mom, then shifted as he took in the look on her face.

Mom was starry-eyed and a little unfocused. Her hands were moving in her lap, twitching to one side and the other like they were warming up for a marathon stint of chores. "Landscapers," she said absently. "Painters and ironwork restorers. First impressions are the most important, you know. That broken window needs immediate tending." And she trailed off, lost in her own world of house restoration.

The house had seen better days, sure, but couldn't his parents see its potential? As far as Oliver was concerned, his feeling about Silverton Manor was growing stronger by the minute.

Poppy yanked open her door before Dad even turned off

the engine, and Oliver followed her across the driveway. Car doors slammed as the others clambered out behind them.

"Wow," Oliver breathed.

"*Wow*?" Poppy said, spitting the word out like an over-cooked brussels sprout. "*This* is our new place? Really?"

"I think it looks mysterious," Oliver said. "And totally awesome."

"If by *mysterious* you mean creepy, and by *awesome* you mean falling apart in the worst way," Poppy said. But Oliver noticed that she was pretty quick to take off around the side of the house, probably looking for an open back door so she could be the first one inside.

The twins, meanwhile, were running in circles around Rutabartle, who had been leaning next to his car while the Days took in their new surroundings. "Our house! Our new house!" JJ chorused. "Let's all go in!"

Rutabartle's hands shot up in the air and he wobbled, fighting for balance. Oliver couldn't figure out what was going on until he saw that Rutabartle held the old-fashioned skeleton key to the front door. But going up against JJ was to play a losing game. "Let us in!" they clamored, and Joe started jumping in place like a key-hungry piranha. Junie, meanwhile, was innocently bending down to poke around the ground by the town official's shoe. There was something in her hand, and Oliver was immediately suspicious.

"We need the key!" Joe yelled. "We can do it! We're great door openers!"

Finally Rutabartle let out a loud groan and lowered his hands, reluctantly thrusting the key at them. Joe nabbed it and Junie followed him as they shot up the steps toward the front door.

"They are quite the little dervishes, those two," Dad said, shaking his head fondly.

Rutabartle looked like steam might billow from his ears at any minute, but he composed himself with effort. "Well. Let us move on to the important matters we have to discuss, shall we? I'm sure you have heard of Silverton Manor's *reputation* around Longbrook. The primary reason you have been hired is to help restore that tarnished image. And so the thing to remember, as you get settled," he said, his voice casual and conversational, "is the need to act as normal as possible." Deliberately straightening his sunglasses, he took a big stride across the paving stones.

His right foot shot ahead; his left foot stayed stuck in place.

Rutabartle toppled face-first, like a felled tree.

A giggling titter erupted from inside the half-open front door.

"Junie! Joe!" Mom called reprovingly after them, while Dad bent over to help Rutabartle extract his shoe from the paving stone, to which Junie had apparently fastened it with super-sticky bubble gum. Oliver sighed. It sure hadn't taken JJ long to get up to their tricksy ways!

Oliver couldn't feel entirely sorry for Rutabartle, though.

Something about that guy gave him the creeps. If anyone needed to be pranked, it was Rutabartle.

The man's biggest concern right now appeared to be his sunglasses, which had gone spiraling across the ground when he fell. They were extra fancy, with embellished frames and some kind of a Bluetooth phone device built into the side. Rutabartle was polishing the lenses with a soft cloth, puffing and blowing on them, lifting them up to the light as if to make sure all was in tip-top running order. After a moment he replaced them on his nose, adjusted them with care, and turned toward Dad.

"I was just beginning to speak," he resumed, clearly intending to act as if nothing had happened, "about acting *normal*." Placing one arm around Mom's shoulders and the other around Dad's, he started walking them toward the front door, with just the slightest pause each time his still-faintly-sticky shoe connected with the ground.

Oliver had been ready to head off and explore, but something in Rutabartle's tone stopped him short. Why was the man so hung up on things being *normal*? Something about that seemed, well, not quite normal. It also seemed like something that could have an effect on all their lives.

Scurrying quietly after the adults, Oliver kept close and paid attention to Rutabartle's words.

"As I began to say, you will undoubtedly have heard that Silverton Manor has been the victim of some, ah, unfortunate rumors—and completely false ones, I might add."

"The house is haunted!" chirped Joe.

"And cursed!" said Junie. They were standing in the open front door, hands on their hips and eyes gleaming with excitement.

Rutabartle steamed. "*That* is precisely the kind of dreck I have hired you to dispel. It's long past time these scurrilous rumors are put to rest. The house is not *haunted*! And the Silverton Curse? What could be more laughable! But you will find many townspeople who have completely swallowed this blather. Thus, you see the importance of my plan: by witnessing a family—such a *normal* family, with . . ." He paused and frowned slightly, then continued a little too quickly, ". . . very normal children—well, I should think those rumors will be forgotten in no time. Wouldn't you say?"

"Hmm, yes, and you'll send all the necessary repair and restoration people? At your agency's full expense?" Mom had a notebook in hand, scribbling furiously what Oliver was sure was the start of a multipage, fully annotated to-do list, which no doubt meant lots of work ahead for him and Poppy.

"Yes, yes. I have already contracted with a landscaping company, and they will begin reconstructing the grounds next week. You may inform me of anyone else you wish to hire, and with my approval they can have full rein as needed. As agreed upon, I've already had the place set up for wireless Internet."

The three of them moved inside the house and Oliver trailed behind them up the stairs.

"There's a calendar in every room!" Mom exclaimed, poking

her head inside a door. "And every one of them fifteen years old. It certainly has been a while since this house has been lived in, Mr. Rutabartle."

"Naturally," the town official replied. "This is why you've been hired."

"There is a lot of work to be done," Mom continued. "But I'm up for the challenge. We all are."

"Next April," Dad said thoughtfully. "That's the date you've set for the auction?"

Rutabartle waved a hand. "Give or take, you know. I can be flexible at this point, though I do wish to turn the property around as promptly as possible. Six months should be long enough to restore the image of the house. As you can imagine, current interest in the property is limited at best. With your help, I'm sure we can bring this sale to a much more satisfying conclusion."

Mom seemed to come to a decision. "I think perhaps we'll start with a party," she said. "A combination housewarming, getting to know the townspeople, introducing ourselves, and so on. A Halloween party, I'm thinking. Isn't this house just right for it? And with Halloween only two weeks away. How perfect!"

Rutabartle frowned. "I don't think that is quite the impression—"

"Nonsense!" Mom flipped a page on her notepad and started scribbling. "It's *exactly* the right impression. People will see those rumors are just part of the house's charm and mystique. Everyone loves a haunted house on Halloween, don't you think?"

"Well, I'm not sure—" began Rutabartle, but it was obvious that Mom wasn't waiting for his approval.

"Excellent. We've only got a couple of weeks and there's a lot to do, so we'd all best get busy." And she zipped off down the hallway, with Rutabartle fast on her heels. JJ clattered away in the distance, probably planning some new and spectacularly evil prank, and Poppy had disappeared. Oliver stood next to his dad in the huge entrance area. Under its thick coat of dust, the dark wood floor was heavy and smooth. The staircase with its fancy marble banister curved invitingly out of sight, like a finger beckoning him to come. On the walls were oil paintings and one very tall vase with Egyptian-looking etchings.

Six months didn't seem nearly long enough to inhabit a place like this. It was the kind of house you wanted to take your time to explore, savoring every room and introducing yourself to each doorframe and wall hanging. It was the kind of house you wanted to make friends with slowly, because you knew it would be a friendship worth keeping, one that could last a lifetime.

Years and years ago, almost as far back as Oliver could remember, the Days had been a normal family, and Dad had had a normal job as a tax accountant. But one day, as Dad told it, he had accidentally walked into the wrong convention center and had come out reborn into a brand-new career. For the last six years, Dad had been working hard to make it big with his online puppet show, The Jolly Marzipans. The side job of being professional long-term house-sitters had fit perfectly well with Dad's new life goals. Which was all well and good for a while. But Oliver was tired of constantly packing and unpacking and moving and getting to know new places and trying to make new friends over and over, as often as once or twice a year. More than anything, he wanted a home of their own, someplace they would never have to leave.

And now . . .

This was it, Oliver thought. Silverton Manor was the house he had been waiting for, looking for, hoping to find someday. Something big and warm surged inside him. He had come home.

"We've got to find a way to stay in this house," Oliver whispered to himself. "We've just got to. *I've* got to."

Chapter 5

Dahlia couldn't keep the smile off her face as she watched the door shut behind the last member of the Day family. All these living people! In her house! It had been so many years since anyone had lived here that she almost didn't know what to do with herself.

"We've got company!" she crowed, twirling in circles around Mrs. Tibbs. "And they're staying all the way until spring. Think of all there will be to do here now. And there are kids too. This day is just *too* good to be true!"

Mrs. Tibbs had her head inclined to the side. "Well, my gamboling gumdrop, so long as they are settling in, perhaps we ourselves should settle in with some hands-on training in the finer art of ghosting. Do you have any lookout places of a certain height?"

Dahlia beamed. "I know just the spot." She drifted back the way they'd come, through the manor wall and out toward the property's forested edge. "After my cubby, this is my second-favorite place," she confided. "I've never had anyone I could show it to before."

Mrs. Tibbs zipped along behind Dahlia toward a tall oak tree with rough, leaf-stripped branches jutting out to each side.

"Well, I do say," exclaimed Mrs. Tibbs, striking a jaunty pose and propelling herself upward in a standing position. "Have you ever seen a tree that looks better for haunting?"

"It's perfect, isn't it?" said Dahlia, grinning. She couldn't manage the same pose as the older ghost, nor could she rise in place without moving her body. That was a trick she *had* to get Mrs. Tibbs to teach her the moment she got the chance. But for now, she went with the usual: churning a little whirlwind and then hopping from gust to gust, getting to the topmost branch with a spin and flourish.

Only to find that Mrs. Tibbs was still hovering halfway up the tree trunk. "What are these etchings?" she asked curiously.

Dahlia felt her cheeks heating up. "Oh, don't mind those—they're just something I do to . . . pass the time. You know."

"Are these star charts?"

"I've always loved astronomy," Dahlia confessed, sinking back down next to Mrs. Tibbs. "It's something I know about, the sky, the stars—something that never goes away. The stars' positions change, but they're always predictable."

"So you carved these charts in the bark? There must be dozens of them!"

"Well, Mrs. Silverton—my mother—lived and breathed her calendars. She kept dozens of them, in just about every room. And me . . . well, I don't know all that much about *who* I was. So it always seemed important to be able to remember *when* I was."

Mrs. Tibbs ran a finger over the careful sketches, the meticulous night-sky impressions that Dahlia had spent so many lonely hours carving into the side of her tree.

"Once my mother went away," Dahlia said, "there was no one to change the calendars in the house anymore. So I needed another way to keep track of the days and years. We used to watch a lot of astronomy shows on TV together, you know. Or as together as we could be, anyway, between living and ghost. I suppose this was my way to try and recapture some of that. But the stars . . . I can't seem to get enough of them."

"And this way you've been able to track the passage of time. Fascinating!" Mrs. Tibbs's tone was full of admiration, and Dahlia felt her face grow warm again.

"It's nothing, really," she said quickly. "Should we get on with our lesson?"

With a nod, Mrs. Tibbs shot up the rest of the way. Lifting her skirt, she folded her lean legs over the uppermost branch and settled the carpetbag on her bony lap. Dahlia raised an eyebrow. Was that ghost really *sitting* on the branch? The more she watched, the more things there were to learn. Mrs. Tibbs was already talking, though, so Dahlia found a wind pocket next to her and curled up to listen.

"... the house," concluded Mrs. Tibbs. "Do you see what I mean?"

"Hmm," Dahlia mused, hoping she sounded convincingly thoughtful, not quite ready to admit that she'd missed the first part of the speech. "I suppose so. But you might explain it once more, to be sure I've got it right."

"I call it Clearsight, though I'm sure the Ghouncil has some formal term for it. I never can quite keep track of all their fancy names ..." She faltered. "Of course, you won't know about the Ghouncil, will you? Officially, the Spectral Investigative Council, but who wants to chew that mouthful all day long?"

"The Ghouncil," said Dahlia thoughtfully. "They're like ... the ghost police?"

"You could say that. Police and congress and government all rolled into one. Fire department too, I'd reckon." Mrs. Tibbs chuckled. "My, er, bosses, you might say. There's a call for a Liberator and the Ghouncil sends the directions to my Pin and I'm off! But as I was saying: Clearsight. It's a way to get past all the clutter you find in the living world. So, take a good look back at the house."

Dahlia tilted her head and inspected Silverton Manor. She studied the four stories and the turrets. She saw walls and windows, balconies and rough-shingled rooftops. A dozen windows winked like giant eyes. She turned back to Mrs. Tibbs, who was gazing at her expectantly.

"Well?"

Dahlia looked again. "What am I supposed to see?"

"Why, the big picture, of course! What *do* you see?"

"I see a house."

"Yes, of course you see a house, child! But keep on going. Don't stop at the front wall . . . look further, *into* the house."

Dahlia's eyes widened. She could easily pass through objects; why had she never thought of deliberately *looking* through them too? They sure seemed insubstantial enough to start with! It took her more than a few tries, and much coaching from Mrs. Tibbs. But after long minutes of eye-crossing effort, the walls finally brushed away to a ghostly shell, leaving the first layer of rooms clearly visible. Seizing upon her success she kept going, tunneling her vision until, to her amazement, she could see a panorama of the entire house. Each room looked outlined in Christmas lights, with the people inside resting on walls and floors of tracing paper. In one glance Dahlia could see everything that was happening all over the house.

"Well, knock me over with a feather," she breathed.

Each member of the new family was like a figure in a life-size dollhouse—the father lugging suitcases down the hall toward the master bedroom; the mother leaning halfway out of a lower kitchen cupboard, emitting horrified yelps at whatever she'd found in there; a boy around Dahlia's age and a slightly younger girl racing each other down the hallway that led to the upper turret and yelling about who would get to claim that room; and the little twins bopping up and down on a sheet-covered couch like a pair of jumping beans. In between were countless empty rooms, and at the very top of the house was the attic, curiously dark and gray compared to the rest of the house. It felt almost rotten, stewing in the upper part of the house like a bad spot on a potato. But Dahlia was too entranced to give much thought to one sour room.

"I'm starting to get what you mean about the house being a walnut," she said, shaking her head slowly. "Who knew that changing your perspective could make such a difference in what you see!" Dahlia wanted to keep playing with this new Clearsight, but Mrs. Tibbs's face was drawn up into a serious look, which told Dahlia that instruction was on the way.

"The time has come," said Mrs. Tibbs, "to make plans about how we are going to get you Liberated."

"Oh, yes!" Dahlia cried. "And I think the first thing I need to know more about is being Anchored. What exactly does it mean? How does it work?"

Mrs. Tibbs considered. "You know how you like to catch objects as they expire, and hold them here?"

Dahlia nodded.

"Well, in much the same way, ghosts can become Anchored when their death involves unfinished business. When that happens, it's like the object—your Anchor, that is—catches and holds on to you. Then you cannot leave the place where that object is."

"Can't leave that place . . . ever?"

"No, not forever—just until you're loosed," said Mrs. Tibbs. "And that's where I come in. A Liberator can help you examine your memories and find the object that's trapped you. Once that Anchor is found you can release its store of memory, which looses its hold, and then—eureka! You are freed to move on."

"But, Mrs. Tibbs, I don't remember any objects. I don't remember *anything* from when I died."

"Hmmm, then I suppose we shall have to indulge in some good old-fashioned treasure hunting. Wouldn't you say?" Mrs. Tibbs shifted position on her branch. "And I've still got a trick or two up these voluminous sleeves, my dear, which I think you will quite enjoy."

Dahlia looked back at the house. Her little cubby room glowed like a warm beacon, banking the sheet-filled downstairs rooms where she'd spent so many lonesome days and nights. And the upstairs, where she didn't really like to venture, given how the floors got all sucky-gooey and she could never properly rest on them. She knew the house inside out, sure—but only on the surface. She'd put her hands *through* just about every drawer, surface, and hidden nook and cranny. But in all those things she'd never been able to touch or hold, might there be clues to her forgotten past? Somewhere deep inside herself Dahlia began, very quietly, to hope.

"Well, my dear," said Mrs. Tibbs. "I suppose we had better get started. We have a rollicking big job ahead and, very likely, not quite enough time to do it."

From the courtyard below came the sound of an engine starting up. The town official had stuffed himself and his bushy mustache and gleaming sunglasses into his sports car and was calling last-minute instructions out the window. There was something greasy about the man that made Dahlia want to run a squeegee across her eyeballs every time she looked at him.

"—leave you to get settled in," he was saying. "I will probably be around from time to time, checking up on things. Don't mind me, I'll just barge in and around as necessary. You have my number to arrange for repairs, and the landscapers should be on their way shortly."

The engine revved loud enough to drown out whatever Mr. Day was saying from the front porch, but Rutabartle didn't seem especially bothered. He waved his hand briskly, then pulled it in the window and performed a sharp rotation, leaving a wide swath of bare ground in the gravel driveway.

"Well," said Mrs. Day, standing by her husband with hands firmly on her hips. "I can't say I'm sorry to see him go."

"He's gone! He's gone! PLAYTIME!" the twins managed to yell in perfect sync. They were like a little Greek chorus, predicting future chaos and tragedy to come. Dahlia loved them already.

"We certainly have picked an action-filled day to begin our search, haven't we?" said Mrs. Tibbs with a quirk to her lips. "Let us go along inside. There is so much more to ghosting than you could possibly imagine, my glorious gal. And I can positively guarantee that you will love learning it nearly as much as I will love teaching it."

With a bob of her chin, Mrs. Tibbs rippled the air currents

in front of her into a long sheer staircase leading from the tree branch right down to the ground. She crooked her elbow and leaned toward Dahlia, who took the proffered arm eagerly. The two ghosts marched down the invisible stairway, heading toward Silverton Manor and all the hidden mysteries to come.

Chapter 6

And—that's *another* win for me!" yelled Poppy, triumphantly pushing the chocolate bowl closer to Oliver. Death by Chocolate was their favorite way to settle arguments, a game of dueling dice throws where the goal was to throw the lowest count, and where the loser had to eat his score in chocolate. "That's seven more squares for you!" Poppy looked almost ready to roll across the floor in glee. Oliver should have known better than to try to beat Poppy out of anything she really wanted. And she *really* wanted this turret bedroom.

"Dig in, big brother," Poppy said. "Or do you yield?"

Oliver sighed. It was a great room, hexagonal rather than round, with tall windows and a ceiling that went up and up. A spiral staircase wound from the center of the room down to the lower floors. He gazed at the seven chocolate squares stacked neatly in front of him, then up at his sister. She rubbed her stomach and made encouraging munching noises. Oliver

gagged. The game could last as long as the players were willing to eat their losing chocolate piles. They had been eating
for over an hour already. And Oliver knew he just couldn't
stomach another bite.

"Fine," he said. "You win."

"Yes, yes, yes, yes, YES!" Poppy crowed, pumping her fist
in the air and strutting around the room with so much enthusiasm that Oliver was almost glad she had won. He wanted
this room, but she *really* wanted it.

Mom's voice wafted up the staircase. "Lunchtime! Grilled
cheddar-and-Nutella sandwiches in the kitchen!"

All eighty-seven of Oliver's losing chocolate squares
rose in his throat, and for a second he thought he'd have to
make an embarrassing dash to the bathroom—now *Poppy's*
bathroom—but he crossed his eyes and focused on the windowpane directly across from him, and the moment passed.

He was concentrating so hard, in fact, that he almost didn't
notice the bright-red something zooming up the driveway
outside the window. But once his stomach settled and his eyes
uncrossed, he saw that it had wheels and a windshield and—it
was a car! Another visitor, so soon?

Oliver dashed out of the room, clutching his stomach, and
ran down the spiral staircase. From outside came the screech
of brakes and the disgruntled huff of an engine shifting gears.
The front door was down one more flight of steps at the far
end of the long hallway. Below, Oliver could see his father lum-
bering wearily toward the door, with the air of a man who has

left a piping hot cheese sandwich to grow soggy on his plate. But immediately to Oliver's right was a set of glass doors that opened onto a tiny balcony, just big enough for a boy to stand and turn in a full circle. It seemed like the most useless excuse for a balcony, but at this moment it was perfect. Oliver twisted the old iron knob and pushed the doors open.

Outside, a gust of wind slapped him rudely in the face, reminding him that, despite the sneakily bright sunshine, it was still October. Oliver pulled up the collar of his sweater and stepped outside, leaning against the balcony railing to get a better view of the driveway.

The new vehicle was not, in fact, a car but a very small pickup truck, so violently red it seemed to have been dipped in ketchup. The back was filled with lumpy shapes covered by a matching red tarp and fastened with bungee cords. The truck stopped just below the front steps, the engine shut off, and the driver's door clipped smartly open. The man who stepped out was so tall and thin that when he unfolded himself next to his tiny pickup, he was like a lamppost standing next to a park bench. Oliver wondered how he had fit in there at all.

A lamppost, however, the visitor was not. He sprang into action without a pause, clearing the six steps in a giant bound and sinking his finger into the buzzer.

Dad opened the door a crack and peered out. "Yes?"

The tall man stuck a foot into the opening and jabbed it wide with his elbow. "Mr. Day? Yes, Mr. Day, I presume. Well, well. It's fine to meet you, just fine. Got a call a few minutes ago—happened to be right in the area. Yes, right in the area, just driving around casual-like. I didn't mind dashing right over, you know, have a little look around and see how things are brewing." He cleared his throat and beamed. "I'm a man of action, you see. Like to dive right into a project, I do. I'm Rank T. Wiley of Terminators, Inc. At your service."

With a quick karate-chop movement, the man thrust out his bony hand. Dad hesitated for a second, then shook it. "Yes, I'm Arthur Day," he said, opening the door the rest of the way. "Pleased to meet you. But . . . Terminators, Inc.? What did you come here hoping to *do*, exactly?"

"Ah! I'm delighted you should ask. Mr. Day—Arthur, may I call you Arthur? Yes? Good. Well, Arthur, if you'll look right this way . . ." Wiley's arm snaked out to wrap around Dad's shoulders.

Before Oliver knew what was happening, Rank T. Wiley had Dad down the stairs and they were strolling around the outside of the house, Wiley gesturing as he blabbed on about needed house repairs.

". . . the gutters, you see? Years, clearly, since they've been seen to. Maybe longer! And the siding!" Wiley shook his head. "Of course the wiring will also need a complete overhaul. And have you thought of maintaining your heating system? Essential! Utterly essential! And that's the most paltry of beginnings. I'm fully accredited in each of these areas, as well as equipped to handle plumbing and all other in-house needs."

Oliver groaned. Where was Mom when Dad needed her? At this rate, the weird new arrival would be moved in before the hour was up. Still, there was something fascinating about this Mr. Wiley. And getting renovations started on the house— maybe *their* new house someday, he wished, he *hoped*—so quickly was a great idea. Oliver might have lost the turret room, but as long as his family got to stay in the house in the long run, he would come out of this a winner.

"But . . . Terminators?" Dad said again from below, still sounding confused.

Wiley waved away the question. "A mere figure of speech, Arthur my man. A simple handle. Our company's humble statement of purpose, so to speak. A way of saying that with my arrival, all your problems will be gone . . . poof! Er, terminated. In the twinkling of an eye." Wiley struck a dramatic pose, presumably so that Dad might witness the aforementioned twinkling eye.

A sudden look of relief broke over Dad's face. "Oh!" he exclaimed. "I've just realized—you were sent by Mr. Rutabartle, weren't you? He did say he would be calling for support staff, didn't he? Am I remembering that right?"

Wiley's pause was so slight that Oliver figured he must have imagined it—it was there and gone, then the man was nodding his head vigorously. "That's it exactly—good man, Rutabartle. Terminators, Inc. First company to call in a crisis, that's the word on the street. Sent me right on over here, zip zip."

"Ah, well, that explains it. I never imagined he would be so very quick and efficient. But people do surprise you! I suppose I'd better let you get started then, Mr. Wiley." Immediate mystery solved, Dad was now casting longing looks back in the general direction of the lunch table.

Wiley, however, swiveled his head mournfully from side to side. "Such an extensive project, though." He squinted at the midday sun. "Seems like no sooner would I get the tools unloaded than it'd be time to put them away . . ."

Dad cocked his head. "You want to come back tomorrow?"

"Quite a large place you have here. It seems to me, if a worker had a place to stay for the duration of the job, he might be able to squeeze a good deal of extra work in those morning-to-evening hours . . ."

Dad frowned.

"Big house like this, an extra body probably wouldn't even be noticed. Apart from the busy *tap-tap-tap* of the hammer, that is. The *swish* of progress. The *zoom* of updated innovations being introduced into a warm family abode." There was a pause, then Wiley reached into his pocket and pulled out an envelope. "You're probably thinking safety concerns, am I right? Well, you can set your mind at ease with this packet. References! Notarized recommendations! Verification phone numbers! Everything you could possibly want for checking up on an unexpected in-home expert." The man took a step back and folded his arms.

Oliver grinned and waited for his father's inevitable invitation. At their last house-sitting job, they'd had a family of Icelandic immigrants packed into the parlor for nearly three weeks while the parents got back on their feet. The youngest was a marble shark who'd cleaned out Oliver and Poppy's prize collection before they finally saw the family on their way. Mr. Wiley, though, would at least be a useful houseguest.

"Well, that sounds like a fine idea," Dad said, leafing through the papers and growing more confident as he read on further. "Quite fine. It's settled then. There is quite a spacious guest bedroom on the far side of the ground floor, past the mudroom. There's even a private back-door entrance. If you'll move your things in there, you can stay for the duration of the job. Marsha won't mind, I'm sure. And now, Mr. Wiley, I must get back to my lunch while it remains passably edible. Shall we resume this conversation in a few hours?"

"Very certainly, Arthur," Wiley beamed. "An absolute pleasure doing business with you."

Dad was up the stairs almost before Wiley had finished his sentence, leaving the door cracked open behind him.

Oliver watched from his upper vantage point as, left alone outside, Wiley strode along the narrow path surrounding the mansion. The man's head twisted in all directions like a curious owl. What was he doing now? Oliver leaned out over the railing to get a better look. Wiley reached inside his jacket and pulled out a long skinny instrument—like a TV remote, but three or four times as long. It was made of a metal so black that it seemed to suck in the light from anything near it. With a quick scurry, Wiley disappeared around the corner of the manor.

Oliver looked down at the shiny red pickup truck. A slick company logo was stuck onto the outside door panel. It showed a wavy, amorphous-looking blob behind prison bars, as if the logo were saying, "Hire me and all your blobs will go away!" Maybe the blob was supposed to stand for all the many problems Wiley's company would fix for his customers? Underneath the logo were the words "Terminators, Inc." There was something odd about the placement of the words, but Oliver couldn't quite figure what.

"Oliver! Your lunch is oozing!"

Soggy cheddar-and-Nutella sandwiches were one of the few things that consistently gave Oliver nightmares, so he needed no further persuasion—especially now that all the action was over outside and the last of his chocolate battle digested.

Closing and locking the balcony door, Oliver headed downstairs, still thinking of the oddball visitor with the weird logo and that device he was so eager to start using. Oliver *had* to find out more about Rank T. Wiley's plans.

Chapter 7

There's something sneaky about that new fix-it man," Dahlia observed, glancing back over her shoulder at the pickup truck as she ghosted through the side wall.

"He certainly talks a blue streak," agreed Mrs. Tibbs. "But let us not be diverted. If we are going to begin the search for your Anchor, there are a few techniques you will need to master first."

"Oh, yes!" Dahlia said. "I've been watching you very carefully, you know. I can already tell that I'm a terrible ghost. Just think—for years and years I've been dead, and now I find I've been going about it all wrong. What can I do, Mrs. Tibbs? Will you show me the real rules of ghosting?"

"Ah, my gifted gollywhopper!" She shook her head. "The Ghouncil has built a whole empire around their rules. Yes, there are certainly plenty of those to go around. Of course," she said hastily, "that's not to say that they aren't important, in their own way. And you will certainly learn them all in due time. However, I see no indication that you have been wasting your time here, nor going about things poorly. I dare say that you have built up a most satisfactory existence."

The words kindled a warm glow in Dahlia's middle, but before she could reply, Mrs. Tibbs clapped her hands together. "Now, all code-correct Ghosting procedures will be taught to you when you complete your Crossover. What we must focus on at this precise moment is finding your Anchor. And to do that?" She jutted her right arm straight up into the air, finger outthrust. "You must learn the Rules of Contact! Like most essential things in life, these are extraordinarily simple: To make Contact, you must only remember to Clear and Concentrate."

Dahlia waited. When Mrs. Tibbs didn't say more, she said, "Wait—that's it? That's all I have to do? But what does that *mean* exactly?"

Mrs. Tibbs clucked. "All right, there is a *little* more to it than that. But it does become second nature after a while, I promise. Let me demonstrate." They were in the living room now, which was mostly draped in sheet-covered furniture. Only one ornate burgundy couch had been uncovered, the white sheet wadded up and muddy-footprinted in a way that hinted that the uncoverers were quite likely small and up to no particular good.

Dahlia hovered above the couch, squirming. "I hate the whole *sinking in* part—I just hate it! That's why I never stay long on the upper floors. It's so easy to lose track of myself and fall right through things."

"But what about your tree carving?" asked Mrs. Tibbs. "You were able to make Contact there, weren't you?"

"Well, yes, I suppose so." Dahlia hadn't thought of that. "I haven't been able to affect anything else, though. Living objects are mushy. I can't touch them or pick them up or sit on them or anything."

"Why do you suppose that is?"

"I've got absolutely no idea. *Should* I know?"

Mrs. Tibbs slid smoothly over until she was above the couch. Pulling herself into a sitting position as straight as a capital L, she lowered herself with dignity onto its cushioned surface. Dahlia's mouth dropped all the way open. "Gosh, that's something else! I can even see it squishing under you. Good work, Mrs. Tibbs!"

"Tut-tut, my dear. It's nothing at all! Now, how about you describe your carving process to me."

Dahlia pondered. "I just—well, I sort of"—she grinned—"I sort of sharpen up my finger into a point. I don't know how it works, only that it does. I usually make a chart when the stars are sitting heavy on my heart. They fill me up and up until I just have to let them out. Then I go to my tree, lean in to the bark, and draw what I see." She looked up. "Does that help at all?"

"It sounds to me like you have been practicing your Clear and Concentrate without realizing you were doing so. Now, why don't you try to grab ahold of those same feelings and take a seat over here next to me."

Dahlia did a little flip and hovered in the air next to Mrs. Tibbs. She tried to clear her mind, though she could feel it wobbling like a ghost flower in a breeze. Slowly, ever so slowly, she lowered herself toward the see-through surface of the unexpired couch.

And sank in to her waist.

"Ack!" she yelped. Her backside prickled like it was being stuffed with cotton.

Mrs. Tibbs smiled. "Never you mind, my graceful gadabout. Time and practice will get you there in the end. Keep your mind on the rules: Clear and Concentrate. First, Clear your mind: scrub it all the way out. Any heightened emotion will get in your way—above all you must be master of your internal senses."

Dahlia focused on emptying her mind. Her excitement and her frustration pretty much canceled each other out, and she pushed them firmly aside. She could do this. She *would* do this. She focused until the couch sat right in the center of her mind, blocking out everything else.

"And now, Concentrate. Think carefully about what you're doing. See in your mind an image of yourself sitting on—*on* the sofa, resting your full self . . ."

Dahlia squeezed her eyes shut and imagined herself following the instructions. She felt no difference, but when she looked down again she gave a cry of surprise. "Look, I'm doing it! I'm sitting *on* the couch. It's so easy—like I'm not even trying!"

With that, Dahlia lost her focus and fell through the bottom of the couch, so fast and hard that she cleared the wood floor and was halfway into the foundation before she was able to stop herself. Shooting back up with a mouth tasting of expired dust bunnies, she quivered with delight.

"I think one might call you a victim of your own success," Mrs. Tibbs said upon seeing her face, which Dahlia knew was beaming like an electric lightbulb. "You must learn to contain your excitement if you want to hold on to your progress!"

"Never mind all that," Dahlia gushed. "I did it! I did it once and I'll do it again. Dust bunnies be gone, my rear will no longer be stuffed with fluff. Or not for long, anyway." She giggled. "Can I go start practicing now? Give me a couple of hours, Mrs. Tibbs, and I'll be a Contact *expert*. I want to be able to touch *everything* in this place!"

"I think that sounds like a capital idea. If there is a better time than the present for beginnings, I'm sure I've never found it."

Dahlia was already busy at work: focusing, clearing, toppling halfway through all sorts of substances. Many were ones she'd never fallen into before, and over the course of tumultuous minutes she learned that porcelain has a far creamier residue than plain old glass; that those candlesticks her mother had been so proud of were not, in fact, made of pure silver; that the warmth of sunlight pooling on an old carpet counterbalanced its musty gruff overtones so that it felt like a scratchy bubblebath.

She was just starting to get the hang of this technique when a loud slam from the rear of the house diverted her attention. "Did you hear that?" she said to Mrs. Tibbs, who had been watching her with amused satisfaction. "Who could it be? We should go investigate!"

Mrs. Tibbs murmured agreement and Dahlia took off like a shot. She slipped through two or three walls before coming to the source of the noise. It was a large bedroom with an old fireplace in the corner and a door leading to the outside. Next to the door was a pile of boxes and jumbled machinery that had obviously been recently brought in.

"The guest bedroom," Dahlia said to Mrs. Tibbs. "I suppose this is where they're putting that Wiley guy. Mrs. . . . my mother always kept this room done up, even though I don't remember anyone ever staying in here." She frowned. "She always put a chocolate on the pillow when someone was coming over."

There was no chocolate on the pillow now, but a neatly folded pile of bedding rested on a chair next to the door. Obviously someone had already been in to make Mr. Wiley feel welcome. But then a flicker of motion caught Dahlia's eye, standing out like a spotlight in this see-through room of living people. It was the blur of something about to expire.

"What do you see?" Mrs. Tibbs asked curiously.

Dahlia wasn't sure at first. It was something small,

something . . . "A pillow-chocolate!" she squeaked. And then she dove—a spectacular dive, full-body, head forward toward the floor beneath the chair. At the last minute she remembered the rules, focusing her ghost breath to clear her mind and concentrate on the hard oak-board surface, so that as she landed she glided smoothly across it. She squished her ghost-body up into a twisty noodle that slid right between the chair legs, only slipping into the floor the tiniest bit at the end. And there it was: caught between the back chair leg and the heating vent was a small square of chocolate, half-melted, nearly flattened out of existence.

Perfect.

Dahlia had to wait only a second or two while the last edge of the chocolate nugget pulled loose from the wreckage of its living form. She had just snatched the expired treat when the vent next to her began to hammer so loudly that she jumped and lost her focus, sinking all the way down into the grainy wood floor.

Gritting her teeth, she shot up through the chair. Mrs. Tibbs hovered about, looking concerned. "Are you all right, ghost child?"

"I'm fine," she said, panting a little. "Just lost my balance there for a minute. But look what I got!" She waved her prize under Mrs. Tibbs' nose.

"You don't mean that you . . ."

"Don't you ever eat expired food, Mrs. Tibbs?" Dahlia grinned, feeling quite giddy at being able to show the well-informed Liberator a new trick. "I'm starting to think I'm a bit of a rebel! Well, I'm happy to say that there's quite enough for two."

"Oh!" The Liberator's eyes went a bit melty. "My gorgeous ghoul, do you know how long it's been since I've tasted chocolate?"

"I can guess. So let's not wait a second longer!"

They munched in companionable silence for a minute, until Dahlia said, "I think chocolate should have a double-expired form, don't you?"

"Mmm, quite," said Mrs. Tibbs, licking the last drips from her fingers. "A regenerating chocolate spirit, wouldn't that be just the ticket."

Dahlia sighed in contentment and wafted over to the pile of luggage by the door. As she did so, there was a clatter on the step outside and the door burst open. It went right through Dahlia, leaving her dazed and a little breathless. She scooted back so as not to be socked by Wiley himself entering the room. Things had never been this difficult when her mother was still around, she thought peevishly. Even though Mrs. Silverton had never sensed Dahlia's ghostly presence, at least she hadn't barreled around irresponsibly, crashing through her at all times.

Wiley, meanwhile, seemed to be in a fine mood. "Now now, my little ghosties," he purred. Dahlia startled, scooting back along the wall alongside Mrs. Tibbs.

"Ahem," said the Liberator, her wrinkled cheeks quivering

slightly. "Our new fix-it man is more sly even than we'd suspected. In fact, I would be mighty surprised if he *is* a fix-it man."

"What do you mean?"

"Do you see all that equipment?"

Dahlia did see, but it didn't mean anything to her in particular. There weren't any traditional-looking tools—just an assortment of devices and machines with huge speakers and something that looked like a poorly assembled vacuum cleaner. Dahlia squinted at a black box that seemed to pulse in the waning afternoon light. "What is that thing?" she whispered.

"Come to me, you fine wee beasties," purred Wiley, and zipped out the door again, slamming it hard behind him.

"That box," Dahlia said, drifting closer.

In a flash Mrs. Tibbs was at her side, catching Dahlia's hand in both of hers. "Don't touch that," she breathed. "Don't even go near it."

"But there's something so wrong . . . Oh, I know what it is—I can't see through it! I know it's a living object. I saw that Wiley guy bring it in. But it's not see-through like everything else. In fact, I can't see through it at *all*."

"That box is lined with a substance called ironite."

"Ironite? What's that?"

Mrs. Tibbs's face darkened. "No one knows for sure where ironite comes from or how it is formed. But the important thing is this: ghosts cannot pass through it."

Dahlia's eyes widened. "Not at *all*?" Some things felt better to pass through than others, some things could even hurt to go through, but she'd never found anything that she couldn't cross at all. "Wait . . . but who would want something like ironite, something ghosts can't pass through—and what would they want it for?"

Then she froze as something caught her eye. On the side of the box was a logo, nearly identical to the one she'd seen on Wiley's pickup truck, but different in one important way. Underneath the wispy white shape, which sat inside the circle with the prison-bar lines down the front, the company name didn't say Terminators, Inc.

It said *Ghoster*minators, Inc.

Chapter 8

Oliver came downstairs to greet the moving truck when it arrived promptly at eight o'clock the next morning. Junie and Joe had been watching for it since sunup, from the vantage point of their new Headquarters of Mischief on the tiny second-floor balcony that Oliver had discovered the day before. They had stowed their Bag of Pranks out there, and that left them just enough room to squeeze in after it. Apparently the view provided lots of inspiration for tricks to play on the wider world.

"Moving truck! The truck is here!" JJ chorused now, bopping mildly in place since there wasn't enough room for their full jumping routine. Then they jostled each other back through the door into the house, where Oliver could hear them thundering down the hallway in the direction of their incoming belongings.

By the time the dust settled in the circular driveway and

the truck's engine had turned off, all six Days were perched on the front steps. The movers, who introduced themselves as Beano and Bob, began to carry boxes inside under Mom's direction, while Dad dug through the back of the truck to find his puppet show crates. He was still stressed about not having brought along his puppets in the minivan, although it would have taken two minivans just to fit the stage, much less all the props and main characters. You don't become an Internet sensation by sticking to the same scenery every time, Dad always liked to say. But then, he still wore the same lucky hat he'd put on the day he started his business, and he said he was wearing *that* until success wrested it off his head.

Oliver snagged his three boxes from the truck, piled them into a tipsy tower, and set off up the stairs. After fully exploring the house—there were eight bedrooms to choose from, after all—Oliver had finally decided on a tiny room all the way at the top of the house. It was just big enough for his bed and dresser, with a narrow sliver of floor besides, but Oliver liked the idea of being so far away from everything and everyone else in the house. This would really, truly be his own private domain. He named it the Matchbox.

The wide, spacious house seemed to shrink to a very small point up there in the attic. Even with the wide-open storage area, the bedroom seemed small for what was left, and he wondered if there might be more junk space closed off somewhere inside the walls. When it came to mysteries and unusual happenings, Oliver figured the more the better. Come to think of it, maybe that was another reason he liked this room.

Unpacking and settling into the Matchbox took less than half an hour. A few of his book boxes were still down in the truck, but Mom had discovered a real library on the second floor and had decreed that all the family's books should go straight there. Which was actually a good thing, since a bookshelf would not have fit in Oliver's new room.

Now finished with setup, Oliver pondered his next move. If he went back downstairs, Mom would put him to work. He decided to go talk to Poppy. He set off down the attic steps and across the winding route to the turret room.

"Poppy!" he whispered, knocking on her door. Living in a turret had its advantages—there wasn't much chance of anyone wandering by and overhearing them. But Oliver still didn't want to risk being conscripted into Mom's forced labor, so he kept his voice down. After a minute or two he heard Poppy clomping down her circular staircase to the landing, and the door opened. She peered out, looked up and down the hallway, then nodded him in.

"Come for more chocolate?" she said, plopping down on her canopied bed and folding her hands in her lap.

Oliver's mouth dropped open. Since he'd been in here yesterday, the room had been completely transformed. He knew that not all girls were girly. Junie, for example, was twice the tomboy Joe was. But Poppy had a deeply felt passion that every surface deserved its own ruffle. Preferably pink and, when possible, combined with flowers and/or lace. She'd been this way ever since Oliver could remember, so he wasn't too surprised at the fate of her room. But this time, she'd come up with a ton of brand-new stuff and had gone all out. Long tentacles of lace oozed from the ceiling, every wall dripped with gauzy fabric, and intricate flowery doilies covered the floor from wall to wall.

Oliver would have been impressed with her speed and thoroughness if he hadn't felt so nauseated by the result. All in all, the room's new look completely succeeded in killing any of his lingering desire for the turret room.

"You wanted to see me?" Poppy said imperiously from her poufy throne-like bed.

Oliver shook the ruffles out of his head and looked around for a clear space of floor. Not finding one, he lowered himself very slowly in place in front of a bright-pink space heater. Pulling his knees to his chest, Oliver got right to the point. "It's about this house," he said. "I want to keep it."

"Wait, really?" said Poppy, sitting up. "You've been looking for the Dream House forever. Now this is it?"

Oliver gave a determined nod. "It's the one, all right. Don't you feel it too? Something like, I don't know, destiny maybe? Like it's meant to be?"

Poppy shrugged. "I feel that way about every house. I'm so sick of having to set up my room all over again every few months."

"That's a start, I guess. But come on, this house is obviously the one. Look at this room you scored! Are you with me on this?"

"Hmm, yeah," Poppy mused. "This place'll do. But look at all I had to put up around here to get the creepy vibe out of the air!" She shivered. "There's something a little weird in this place, if you ask me."

"Hey," said Oliver, standing up. "Don't bad-talk this room. You sure fought hard enough to get it!"

"I love this room," Poppy said quickly. "It's not that. More like the house itself. Like there's something else going on with it, something a little spooky."

"Now you're talking like one of those old Longbrook guys," Oliver said, grinning. "But anyway, spooky is cool, right? So we're agreed. We'll figure out a way to stay at Silverton Manor."

Poppy just shrugged, and that was good enough for Oliver. He could work with that.

"I don't think it's going to be easy," he said. "That Rutabartle guy said they're putting the house up for sale in the spring. Why can't Mom and Dad just buy it, skip over the auction altogether?"

Poppy snorted. "Good luck with that. Mom and Dad couldn't afford to buy a duck pond. Or a duck to live in it. So what's your big plan for staying?"

"I haven't exactly figured that out yet," Oliver confessed. "Let's both do some exploring, gather up ideas, and we can talk about it more later."

Poppy perked up. "We could go explore together!"

"No!" Oliver said quickly. "I think this kind of sneaking, er, works better alone."

"That's not fair!" said Poppy. "You never let me do stuff with you."

"You're noisy," he said.

"And you're mean." Poppy flopped back on her bed, scowling.

Oliver felt bad about shutting down Poppy's plans, but he *definitely* didn't want his little sister tagging around with him all day. Some things were just too awful to bear.

"We'll figure out more plans later, okay?" he said, pausing at the door.

The plush *Princess* pillow hitting the wall beside him was Poppy's only answer.

Feeling vaguely guilty, but no less determined, Oliver tromped back down the turret steps, looking both ways down the hall first to make sure Mom wasn't around. He hadn't seen Wiley for a while, and wondered what project the fix-it guy was tackling first. Oliver thought he'd said something about the plumbing, and he had seemed very busy lugging around some impressive-looking machinery.

As if on cue, there was a low rumble from somewhere in the upper house. It didn't sound like plumbing, though. It almost sounded like . . . a moan? For a second Oliver thought about the stories they had heard about the house in Longbrook. Then he laughed at the way he was obviously letting Poppy's superstitious worries get to him. Ridiculous! And that was when he heard Mom's voice, trumpeting loud and clear—and right around the corner.

"Why yes, Beano, that is original wood. Antique, of course. Yes. One of our last house-sitting jobs—simply a delightful woman. She was scaling back and couldn't keep it all. We got it for a song, I tell you! No, right there. Wait! Yes, just like that. A little more to the right maybe? I've got such a decorating job ahead of me, you have no idea! I'm going with all new drapes, minimal paint because it is *so* messy, but a few classy stretches of wallpaper, because of course—"

Mom was in a mood, there was no doubt about it. Anything not nailed down would be sucked into her vortex of usefulness. Oliver looked around wildly. He had to stay out of sight. Right in front of him was an alcove—a shallow nook in the wall, big enough for an ornate mirror and a fancy end table which had already been topped with a vase full of fresh flowers.

Aha! Mom had already been here. Which meant this nook would be off her radar. She was right at the corner now, maybe two seconds away.

He dropped to the floor and slid under the table, just as Mom swept into view, with two movers behind her lugging their ancient, fiercely ugly grandfather clock. Mom insisted the clock was worth untold riches, but Oliver's toes curled every time he heard its chime. If Mom hadn't been so deep in conversation she would have spotted him for sure, but as it was he pulled his foot out of her way just in time, and only Beano the mover tilted his head and winked as if to say, "Dude, I totally wish could hide under there for a while myself."

And they were gone. Mission accomplished! Freedom secured.

Then Oliver noticed something strange. Right under the rim of the table, at about his eye level, was a tiny blinking red light. The light came from a thumb-sized device. He unclipped it and turned it over in his hand. It looked like a tiny webcam . . . it even had a little lens—and it was turned on. *Broadcasting?* But why, where, and to whom?

There were only two possibilities: either the camera was already in the house when they moved in, or somebody just put it here. But if it had been in an empty house for years and years, would it still be active like this, with the light on?

Oliver had to talk to someone, and fast. Dad knew all about webcams and online stuff. He would know what to do.

Jumping out from under the table, the device clutched firmly in his hand, Oliver scurried down the hallway, his mind racing. This wouldn't give Mom and Dad second thoughts about staying in the house, would it? They'd already been paid half their fee for moving in, and they'd get the rest at the end of the six months. Oliver knew that Dad had invested in new microfiber puppet bodies for the circus troupe that would be joining The Jolly Marzipans in the upcoming Super Online Launch event. No way Dad would want to give that money back, even if he could. But on the other hand, Mom was very big on Safety First. And if someone was spying on them ... that was just beyond creepy.

Nearing the end of the hallway, Oliver was just turning to go downstairs when he heard a scuffling sound. Something tugged hard on the back of his shirt, and he was yanked through an open door that promptly slammed shut behind him.

Somewhere down the long hallway Oliver could hear Mom screech, "What did I say about slamming doors?" But Oliver had no reply to that question. All he could do was gape into the face of Rank Wiley, arms folded and eyes blazing, looking like someone who absolutely should not be crossed. Ever.

Chapter 9

Ghosterminators?" Dahlia was laughing so hard at the weird-looking logo that her fingers and toes were going all wispy. "That's the silliest thing I've ever heard."

But Mrs. Tibbs pursed her lips. "Not so very silly," she said. "I've dealt with this type of agency before. Rank Wiley could mean all sorts of trouble for us."

"Trouble?" said Dahlia. "He's a skinny windbag."

"That may be," said Mrs. Tibbs, "but he has some nefarious plan in mind, if I'm not mistaken. Why else would he change the logo on his truck, removing the word *ghost*? And all that blather about being a fix-it man? I don't believe a word of it." She shook her head. "No, he is up to something, and I'm quite afraid that it has something to do with *us*. I would feel much better if I knew exactly what this Rank Wiley has in mind."

"Well, what are we waiting for? Let's go find out!" Dahlia

tried to remember how to work her new Clearsight skill. It was much harder to do from inside the house—being at a distance gave one an advantage, she supposed—and the effort of focusing on seeing through stuff made her lose hold of her Contact skills.

But as she sank slowly into the floorboards, Dahlia managed to punch her sight out ahead of her—through the guest bathroom, the mudroom, the living room with its sheet-covered furniture. Her gaze was like a lighthouse beam sweeping right through the house. She was momentarily distracted when passing through the kitchen, to see a delicious-looking expired sandwich floating away above Poppy's head—maybe they could zip through the kitchen on their way? She would love to connect with a few bites of expired salami on rye!

But then Mrs. Day glanced around the room. "Where is Oliver? It's not like him to be late for lunch."

Dahlia snapped back on course. She *had* to find that stinky ghosterminator.

She zeroed in on Wiley a few seconds later—and Oliver right along with him. "Come on," she said to Mrs. Tibbs, who sat regarding her with prideful satisfaction. "They're in the boiler room. I'm not sure what's going on, but something's not right in there."

When the two ghosts slipped through the boiler room wall, the first thing they saw was Oliver sitting in a dejected heap on the floor. His head was in his hands. Wiley paced back and forth, waving a hideous pair of goggles that looked like something you'd wear to get your eyesight tested, and apparently coming to the end of a long speech.

"So now I think you can get my drift, comprehend my mission, understand my undertaking, hmmm?" Wiley concluded, waving his arms in a final flourish and stopping just short of taking a bow.

Oliver frowned. "Let me see if I'm getting this right: You believe ghosts are real. You think there are ghosts in this house. You put up cameras to spy on the *ghosts*—not on *us*, you say—but you're lying to my parents about being here to fix up the house. You're not even a handyman. And you don't want me to tell them any of that. Did I leave anything out?"

Wiley bristled. "Lying? Why, nothing could be further from the truth! I am as handy as any man to wear a tool belt, and as for fixing? Pah! I'm Rank T. Wiley, and the *T* stands for *Troubleshooting*. I simply chose to *specialize*, if you will, repairing areas of the atmosphere which are infested with ghostly vermin, purging the specters and restoring the natural balance of the environment." He heaved a dramatic sigh. "I know those cameras might *seem* upsetting, but when seen from a scientific standpoint, the logic is clear. Six of them only, exclusively placed in public, yet out-of-the-way places: attic, cellar, alcoves, and so on. Prime lurking spots for spectral activity. No breach of privacy, no wool being pulled over eyes, nothing like that whatsoever! Just clean, honest-to-goodness ghosterminating." Wiley paused, seeming almost too impressed with himself to go on.

"So why keep what you're doing a secret, if it's all so aboveboard?" Oliver asked.

"That is an excellent question, and the fact is this: I—that is to say, science, humanity, and *the world*—simply *cannot afford* to have these plans thwarted. What I am doing here is too important to risk being turned away. And I think you will agree with me that your town official wants everything around here to be perfectly *normal*." Wiley turned suddenly and narrowed his eyes. "This is the closest I've come to my goal of capturing a bonafide specter, and nothing is getting in my way."

Oliver looked up quickly. "So you've never actually *seen* a ghost?"

"Two full decades I've been focusing on my own brand of in-depth spectral studies, and I'll have you know that I've seen *many* a lair and paranormal hotspot. I could tell stories that would curl your hair and bake your brownies! What I have yet to do is lay my hands on an actual living—or nonliving, to be technical—genuine *ghost.* And that is what I intend to do here."

"I still don't get why you think I won't tell my parents, no matter what you say," Oliver mumbled. To Dahlia's alarm, he didn't sound quite as certain as he had a minute before. Of course he was going to expose Rank Wiley . . . wasn't he?

But an evil grin was spreading across Wiley's face. "Well, from what I have seen and heard since my arrival, you are especially keen on staying in this house, young Oliver. Am I correct, hmmm? And what do you think will happen if your parents discover that this house is haunted by *sinister specters*, *devouring demons*, and *ghastly ghouls*? Does that sound like a safe location to you? Do you really think they would allow their precious darlings to remain in this infernal mansion?"

Oliver opened his mouth, but Wiley cut in quickly. "Don't think I don't have proof," he growled. "Don't think I can't lay out a full scientific case that will send your parents running for the hills!"

Dahlia clenched her hands into fists. "Who are you calling sinister, mister?!" she yelled, knowing perfectly well Wiley couldn't hear her, but too mad to care. Oliver was looking at the ground, and it was clear that the ghosterminator had pegged him right.

Oliver loved this house, she realized. He really loved it, even though he'd just gotten here. For a second Dahlia tried to see the place through his eyes . . . it was rather lovely. But she couldn't help noticing the irony: all Dahlia wanted to do was leave, and all Oliver wanted to do was stay—and this sneaky weasel was getting in the way of both their plans.

"Dahlia, my dear," said Mrs. Tibbs quietly behind her.

But Dahlia was not in a mood to listen. She marched up and shook her ghostly finger in Wiley's face. "Now you hold it right there," she spat. Wiley was still talking as Oliver turned toward the door, his sneaker scuffing against the wall.

"I know you can't hear me, but you need to *leave!*" Dahlia growled with another stern finger-shake. Wiley finished his monologue and curled his lip, shoving the goggles over his head and snapping them into place with a resounding *snick*.

"You need to leave RIGHT NOW!"

Something changed when she spoke those last two words; she could tell that right away. In the process of swinging around, Wiley lifted his head and stared straight through the goggle lenses into Dahlia's eyes. All the blood drained from his face.

"GHOST!" he bellowed. "A ghost! Right here!"

And he fell over in a dead faint.

Time hung by a thread while Oliver looked around wildly. Dahlia was shaking from head to toe. Had the ghosterminator just *seen* her?

"Quickly, child," said Mrs. Tibbs, grabbing her hand. "He'll come around in a second and we should not be here when he does."

Mrs. Tibbs pulled Dahlia through walls and floors and furniture until they hit the cold, clean outside air. The afternoon sun hung lazy in the sky and Dahlia couldn't stop trembling as she sprawled out in the air above the branch of her favorite tree.

"What did I do?" she whispered. "He saw me, didn't he? How is that even possible?"

Mrs. Tibbs swung around to face her. "You can't have known this, my dear, but there is another rule you must be aware of—a most important rule, one of which the Ghouncil takes great notice. There must be no Manifesting to the living."

Dahlia drew a hand across her face. Her nerves were settling now, and she was able to make Contact with the branch and pull herself up into a sitting position. She shook her head. "Manifesting? Do you mean letting the living see you? If it's not allowed . . ."—her eyes went wide—"that means it's possible! Is that what just happened?"

"That treacherous toadstool has some very high-tech equipment, which must have enabled the Manifest. It is a most advanced skill and not technically possible until after Crossover."

"After Crossover? But he saw me! I know he did."

"Through the goggles, yes." Mrs. Tibbs shook her head. "I don't like this. I don't like it at all. The Ghouncil is most persnickety about this particular rule. A ghost's essence is augmented after Crossover and Training, so it would sometimes be technically possible to Manifest then. It's still not allowed, of course. But before Crossover? Never!"

"But—"

"My dear—it is imperative that we stay very far away from that man. He means trouble in the worst way."

Dahlia remembered the dark ironite cube she had seen in Wiley's room. "You're right, Mrs. Tibbs, I know you are. But this *is* an awfully big house. It's not like we have to hide out or anything, right?"

Mrs. Tibbs gave a grudging nod. "We can take care to stay out of his way, I suppose. But one thing's for sure: we need to find your Anchor before too much longer. This process is getting more complicated by the day."

"Yes," Dahlia mused. Part of her couldn't wait to get started, wished they'd begun the very moment Mrs. Tibbs had arrived. But another part wondered if maybe they shouldn't rush things quite so much. There were a *lot* of new things to figure out. And now there was this Wiley business to consider.

Dahlia swept her Clearsight through the house. Mrs. Day was vigorously battling the kitchen floor with an old-fashioned mop, while a scowling Poppy wiped the kitchen table and the twins juggled juice boxes in a far corner. Oliver sat on the front steps munching on a droopy sandwich. Up in a long third-floor room, Mr. Day wrestled a colorful tent the size of a couch, with piles of puppet bodies strewn on the floor around him.

And Wiley? There was no other word for it: he was stalking. With his nose bent down toward the floor like a bloodhound, he held out a long black device covered in knobs and buttons. He seemed to be following some invisible trail, and at the slightest noise or movement he would perk up his head, narrow his eyes, and spin in a full circle before putting his head back down and continuing on.

"What do you think?" Dahlia felt the need to whisper as she watched Wiley, even though they were all the way across the courtyard.

Mrs. Tibbs sighed. "Perhaps we should give him a few

hours. Let him search and find nothing for a bit. He'll let his guard down, believe he imagined the whole thing—they always do, you know—and we can unobtrusively get back to work."

Dahlia nodded, sharpened her focus, and settled more comfortably with her back against—*against,* it wasn't really *that* hard, this Contact business—the trunk of the tree. But as she turned and studied Wiley's steady progress across the downstairs hallway, she thought to herself that he didn't seem like someone who was going to believe he had imagined his ghostly encounter. Nor did he seem like someone who would just let it go.

From her perch high up in the tree, Dahlia watched the chilly October wind whip across the courtyard, lifting leaves and tossing up expired objects in the distance.

In the house, Wiley's machine let out an especially sharp crackle, the air popping around him. Dahlia shivered.

Chapter 10

Oliver spent most of the next morning trying to figure out what to do about Wiley's plans. The ghosterminator hummed with a manic energy. There was a new light in his eye, and Oliver knew exactly what it was: Wiley thought he'd seen a ghost. If he'd been slightly whacked before, what was he now?

Oliver knew he had to take the whole thing to his parents. Wiley had boasted about having mountains of proof, which he had gathered in his many years of ghosterminating. Could that be true? Impossible as the whole deal was, they probably *would* believe Wiley all too quickly. Gullible and impressionable were not the most flattering adjectives to apply to your parents, but in this case, the shoes fit. The one thing Oliver couldn't be sure about was whether they would mind living in a supposedly haunted house. But was he willing to take that risk? What if they *did* just decide to leave?

The other thing was that neither of his parents was exactly

easy to talk to right now. Dad was elbow-deep in his circus show, his lucky hat sitting askew on his head, gearing up for the streaming launch that was set to happen in two weeks—on the very night of their big house party. Last night he'd showed off the brand-new banner ads that he'd plastered across the Internet. Now that Dad had committed to a solid start date, Oliver knew they wouldn't see much of him.

And Mom had now been fully replaced by the notorious Party Zombie Mom, who would stop at nothing to chase down her victims and put their brains to work getting ready for the upcoming party. The kitchen was wallpapered in lists, schedules, timelines, and websites; she'd even installed a fancy SMARTBoard that had nine separate screens. Each screen loaded to a particular website, and Party Zombie Mom kept swishing by at random moments: pulling up recipes, ordering supplies, checking ratings, and other crazy stuff Oliver didn't even care to think about.

In one of Mom's better action plans, JJ had been wrapped in some soft cloth and given a bottle of wood floor polish. They were having the time of their lives shuffling up and down the hallways and in and out of bedrooms, leaving some impressively gleaming hardwood floors behind in their wake. Not to mention staying out of trouble. Oliver hadn't been pranked in quite a while, come to think of it. This new house was good for them too.

"Oliver," Poppy whispered as he caught her eye after breakfast. Party Zombie Mom was half-turned away, a zoned-out look on her face. Poppy gestured at him. "Let's get out of here!"

Oliver leaped up and the two of them slid sideways to the door.

"Hmmm?" Mom said vaguely, and Oliver grinned as he shut the kitchen door behind them.

"That was close," Poppy said with a shudder.

"You know she'll put us to work sooner or later."

"The later the better," said Poppy. "We've just gotta lie low. Which you've been doing lots of, by the way. What are you up to now?"

"Um," Oliver said. What *was* he up to? The Wiley problem had been churning in his head all morning. The phony fix-it guy was up to no good, but he hadn't actually done anything wrong, either. Come on—*ghosts?* He was cracked, of course, but that wasn't a crime. In a flash, the answer came to Oliver: all Wiley needed was someone to keep an eye on him. Make sure he didn't do anything too off. And if anything *did* end up being fishy, well, Oliver would be right there to spot it and sound the alarm.

Simple! He remembered what Poppy had said about the house seeming kind of spooky. She might have some ideas about what to do. But then he'd be stuck with tagalong-sister time. "Just stuff," he said at last. "Boring stuff. You wouldn't like it. I'll see you later."

He turned away quickly and zipped off down the hall, pretending not to see the disappointed look on Poppy's face.

It took him a few minutes to find Wiley, whose equipment had now spilled out of the guest bedroom and into the mudroom. The ghosterminator scowled as Oliver entered. "What do *you* want?"

Oliver swallowed a couple of rude replies. He had to keep on Wiley's good side for this plan to work. "I, uh, thought maybe I could help you out today. I've got some extra time on my hands and, well, four hands are better than two, right?"

Wiley narrowed his eyes.

"Oh, wow!" said Oliver quickly. "Look at all this stuff! What does it do? Where did you get it? Did you invent any of it yourself? Does it help you catch ghosts? Would you tell me all about it, would you?" Oliver felt like a Disney version of an enthusiastic young apprentice, or maybe a member of Sherlock Holmes's gang of kid followers, the Baker Street Irregulars— but to his surprise and relief, Wiley cracked a huge smile.

"Well, now that you mention it, it's something of a fine art, is ghosterminating. One which I've perfected, I might add— dare I say, even mastered."

Hook, line, and sinker, Oliver thought smugly. But he widened his eyes and said, "Ghosterminating!" He stopped just short of adding an "aw, shucks" which might have worked well in a Sherlock Holmes story, but probably would spoil the effect here. "How exactly does it work?"

"Very simple, my boy. This apparatus you see here? It is the most sophisticated equipment available anywhere, for any price. Right here you can see my centerpiece: a breakthrough tool called the Aspirator—you can't find this on the Internet, no sirree!" Wiley picked up something that looked like a vacuum cleaner built into a backpack, with a long neon-orange nozzle and a decidedly ominous air. "I don't mind telling you that I've incorporated a few of my own extra twists into the machinery. And it works like a charm. Simply point the nozzle at the beasts and su-u-uck. All gone—swallows them right up into a sealed compartment inside the pack. Nice and tidy."

Oliver didn't have to work at looking impressed. Whatever this ghost nonsense was, Wiley definitely believed it.

"From there, you press this button right here." Wiley pointed out one of the buttons lined up along the shoulder strap of the Aspirator. "The beings are ejected into a specially sealed container—from which, I will add, they are *not* able to escape. As I said—a fine art! A very fine art indeed."

Oliver still felt slightly ridiculous playing along with this game but, for all its idiocy, this "science" of ghosterminating actually was pretty interesting. "Then what?"

"I take them back to my laboratory." Wiley rubbed his hands together gleefully. "And then we shall see what we shall see, hmmm? What are ghosts made of, I wonder. How is their essence constructed—or perhaps I had best say, *deconstructed*? To take them ever so carefully apart, to open them up, if you will—to analyze and identify each of their ghastly and ghostly components . . . that way lies fame and fortune, my boy, for the happy ghosterminator! Fame and fortune. The very name of the game and, I daresay, the pinnacle of this science to which I have devoted my career."

Wiley's idiocy was clearly trumped only by his greed. Oliver felt slightly sick. "But how do you go about, er, *seeing* them? If there were any—I mean, *when* you happen to find any ghosts, wouldn't they be, like, see-through? You know, invisible? How would you even find them?"

Wiley pounced on this question with glee. "It's a tandem attack, my boy! You've seen my goggles. They're not much to look at—pardon the pun!—but what they do is heighten the eye's natural sensitivity to ghostly phenomena."

"That's what happened yesterday?" Oliver had no idea what Wiley had seen, but for a second back there Oliver could almost have believed the guy had seen *something*. Definitely something . . . but a *ghost*? No way.

"Correct, exactly, and right on the money!" Wiley paused as a little shudder passed through him. "I have to say that sighting caught me off my guard. But I assure you, that was a one-time failure. I will not be caught out like that again, no sirree! But as to your question of transparency, nothing could be simpler. Once I've got the specters in my sights, I use a product of my own invention—I call it phoam. For exposing *ph*antoms, you see." His face split in a wide grin. "It's modeled after the fine stuff of fire extinguishers, but vastly more high-tech. And stored right here in my trusty Aspirator. Spray the phoam on those vermin, and poof! Right in the open, for the naked eye to see."

Oliver shook his head a little to clear it. Wiley believed his craziness so much that it was starting to sound halfway believable!

"And now, are you ready to witness the science of ghosterminating in real-life action?" Without waiting for an answer, Wiley set the goggles back down on a low side table. "I won't use these yet. The first thing you need when launching a ghost hunt is the noble Spectrometer."

Oliver shivered as Wiley whipped out the skinny black device he'd been flashing around the property the first day he'd arrived.

Patting his device lovingly, Wiley flipped the switch and beamed at Oliver. "There, you see these numbers? Right around here—mid-forties—that's average. Normal, non-haunted atmosphere. But look at that needle—see it rise? Great gadzooks! I haven't seen such a reading in—well, in quite a while, I assure you." Wiley's eyes bulged and Oliver leaned over to watch as the needle climbed up, and up, and up.

Finally it hovered near the very top of the narrow screen. "These numbers are *astronomical*. I would say there's a 95 percent chance"—Wiley lowered his voice to a dramatic whisper—"that there is *a ghost in this very room*! Boy, pass me those goggles!"

Oliver didn't have time to even react before Wiley was up, whipping the Aspirator pack onto his back and darting toward the door, like a dog pulling on his leash. Not wanting to be left behind, Oliver grabbed the goggles and slipped them over his own head. They were bulky and uncomfortable, and the effect was like trying to see underwater.

He didn't have time to take them off though, because Wiley was on the move and it was all Oliver could do to keep up. "Hmmm, odd, very odd indeed," the ghosterminator was saying. "Those readings skyrocketed and then, poof! Just disappeared. Almost as though . . ." He stood upright and snapped his fingers together. "Of course! The ghoul is on the move." Wiley spun in a full circle before apparently picking something up on his Spectrometer. He pushed through into the mudroom, the Aspirator knocking against the door in his haste.

Oliver followed close behind, ignoring Wiley's ongoing stream of babble, but studying how the goggles warped the air around him. There was nothing ghostly in sight—not that he'd expected there to be—but through these twisted lenses he could almost imagine there was.

"AHA!" Wiley bellowed, snapping Oliver out of his thoughts. They were standing in the sunroom, and the Spectrometer was lit up like a Christmas tree. "What do you have to say now, eh? We've hit the jackpot!"

Oliver shifted his gaze from the Spectrometer to the place Wiley was indicating. "It's just . . . a wall," he muttered.

"But is it *really*?" Wiley reached over his shoulder and pressed a button on the side of his backpack. A low motor started up on the Aspirator.

Oliver squinted at the wall. *What* was Wiley going on about? There wasn't anything there. He glanced back toward the door. Would Mom and Dad hear the noise and come investi-gate? Or could they really imagine this was all part of Wiley's house-fixing plan?

And then Oliver froze. What was *that*?

In front of the door—for the briefest of seconds—through the smudged and warped glass of the goggles, he'd seen the shape of a girl. A foot-stomping, furious, old-fashioned-dress-wearing, completely *see-through* girl.

Oliver had just seen a ghost.

Chapter 11

"My cubby!" Dahlia shrieked. They'd had a narrow escape earlier, when the ghosterminator had whipped out his Spectrometer and started yammering on about *ghosts in this very room!* Mrs. Tibbs had whisked her away so fast that she'd actually left a body part or two fully behind her. By the time she'd pulled herself back together enough to check up on Wiley with her Clearsight, the bloodhound was back on the trail.

And now he'd found his jackpot.

"We have to stop him!" Dahlia wailed. "All my stuff is in there. You heard him describe that Aspirating business. He'll suck it all up! I'll never see it again."

"We should not be hanging around him to begin with," fumed Mrs. Tibbs. "Remember our plan to *lie low*?"

But Dahlia couldn't leave now. She wrung her hands despairingly and hovered at the edges of the sunroom.

Rank Wiley stood in front of the entrance to her cubby. He

had that weird orange-and-black machine strapped to his back. In his twitching hand, the Spectrometer gave a series of sharp pings. Oliver's mouth gaped open, and he turned his head wildly around the room, like he was looking for something he couldn't quite find. Dahlia couldn't spare a minute for this living boy. Her *cubby*! How many years had she worked to put it all together? She could feel tears starting in the corners of her eyes.

"You see," Wiley yelled over the noise, "*that* is the precise direction of the disturbance, right there." He waved an arm. "There might appear to be nothing in that spot, but my fine apparatus indicates otherwise. Now stand back and watch the Aspirator at work!" He depressed a button on his shoulder strap and the nozzle began to vibrate. He yanked it from its holster, holding it out like a fire hose.

A faint glowing outline appeared over one side of Dahlia's cubby. Oliver gasped. "That's the pilot light," Wiley barked. "You see the infected area now, don't you?"

Behind her, Dahlia felt Mrs. Tibbs's hands close around her shoulders. "My dear, I *really* don't think we should be in this room right now."

Dahlia shrugged her off. "We have to do something!" But what? Maybe she could rescue some of her things! She shot forward and in a second she was inside the cubby, looking wildly around. She only had a few seconds at the most. What could she save?

Wiley centered his aim squarely at the middle of the cubby.

He pressed another button. A cloud of pale green foamy gunk flowed from the end. It ballooned into the air and rushed directly toward her.

"I insist!" said Mrs. Tibbs, shooting up beside her. "We must leave *now*." She seized Dahlia and pulled her back toward the sunroom. In the same instant, the phoam connected with the cubby.

The greenish goo slopped all over her tiny room, turning its crisp, sharp edges dull and washed out. Dahlia squeezed her hands into tight fists. She knew what it meant when something looked halfway erased to her: it meant that it was clearly visible in the world of the living.

There were gasps outside. Both Oliver and Wiley seemed momentarily stunned by what they were seeing.

Mrs. Tibbs was still pulling Dahlia along. They were almost through the last wall. But the phoam oozed toward them.

They were not quick enough.

Dahlia screeched as something cold and slimy connected with her foot. "I'm hit!"

"Pull away," said Mrs. Tibbs, tugging on her arm.

But Dahlia's foot would not pass through the last wall. "The phoam!" she gasped. "It's keeping me from ghosting through. What can I do?"

By now, the entire cubby was encased in phoam. Mrs. Tibbs stood inside the sunroom and so did Dahlia, both off to the side and out of Wiley's range, now that the phoam had settled—all except Dahlia's left foot, which was glommed onto the side of her room, stuck like a gopher halfway into its burrow. Again the dark cube flashed in Dahlia's mind. She pictured herself trapped in the tiny space, unable to get out ever again. What could she *do*?

"The shoe!" exclaimed Mrs. Tibbs suddenly. "It's just on your shoe!"

In the terror of the moment Dahlia was having a hard time thinking straight, but she looked down and saw that Mrs. Tibbs was right. She kicked out hard. The shoe came off and tumbled back into her cubby. Her bare foot slipped through the rest of the wall.

With a rush that was as much relief as speed, the two ghosts shot up through the sunroom ceiling and hovered in the room above, watching the proceedings below in trembling horror.

Rank Wiley crowed in triumph. "You see?" he yelled to Oliver over the roar of the Aspirator. "Now you understand my profession, young Oliver, so vital and yet so misunderstood. Since the very moment you set foot in this house—yes sirree, without even realizing it—you have been living with *ghosts among you*! What do you think of that?"

"We *must* go deeper into the house," said Mrs. Tibbs. The flowers on her hat quivered and even her carpetbag looked poised for flight. "That was a very close call. And we haven't seen the end of it."

"No," whispered Dahlia. "I have to stay and see what happens!" Her fingernails still dug into the palms of her hands, but this was her room—these were her treasures. She couldn't just abandon them.

Slipping back down through the floor, Dahlia circled the far side of the sunroom. She kept to a cautious distance—she had not forgotten her near-Aspiration—but close enough to keep tabs on what was going on.

Rank Wiley fiddled with the knobs on his machine. The loud blowing sound stopped, gurgled, and a harsh sucking noise took its place. Dahlia's stomach flipped over, but she would not leave. Not yet. It couldn't be true—this man couldn't *really* . . . could he?

The nozzle was up again, and Wiley stepped toward the sunroom wall. He took aim. For a few seconds, nothing happened. Dahlia smiled in sudden relief and turned to Mrs. Tibbs. "See? Nothing to worry—" She stopped.

The wall of the cubby was stretching. Like a piece of chewed bubblegum, the nearest wall was getting longer and gooier, slipping steadily toward the nozzle of the Aspirator.

"Nooooo!" Dahlia wailed. Eyes wide, she watched the wall bend and warp until with a loud *thwunck*, it came off in one giant piece. It popped like a bubble and shimmied down into the spout of the nozzle.

The rest of the walls went like a row of dominoes. Then the Aspirator attacked the inside of the room.

Thwunk! One squashy armchair.

Thwunk! Thwunk! Thwunk! One frilly party dress, one well-worn paperback, and a collector's edition of *Curious George*.

Thu-thwunk! A leather left shoe, recently on Dahlia's foot. All vanished into the belly of the Aspirator.

The last bit of ghostly wallpaper disappeared. The Aspirator belched loudly, and Wiley slammed the OFF button.

Outside the sunroom, the wall of Silverton Manor was as bare as a peeled potato. Dahlia's eyes burned with tears, which were suddenly tumbling down her cheeks. Everything she had ever owned, every little bit of the life she had managed to cobble together over her years as a ghost—it was all gone.

It was too much to bear. Dahlia turned and shot through the nearest wall, not knowing where she was going, not caring, not thinking about anything except getting as far as she could from the ruin of her carefully built-up world.

High in the oak tree the minutes stretched like taffy as she hung motionless, not thinking, not feeling, just letting her molecules settle. Had she ever cried before this? She didn't think so. She'd been stuck here in this house for years and years, but it hadn't been so bad. It had been boring sometimes, but there was always *something* she could look at, explore, or do. Her mother had watched a lot of TV—the Discovery Channel mostly, programs about space and stars and planets, which Dahlia loved. Never mind if Dahlia couldn't pass through that stupid Boundary. But the years kept passing, and Mrs. Silverton got older and older, and their halfway-almost conversations—which consisted of her mother talking to the TV, and Dahlia answering, even though she was the only one who could hear herself—had gotten fewer and farther between. And then her mother had left for the nursing home, and that was that.

The house had settled onto itself, growing quieter and more lonely by the day, and Dahlia had started to wonder what else was out there, beyond the Boundary in the greater world. But through all this, at least she'd had her little cubby, her own private nook, somewhere she could be fully *ghost* without having to worry about falling into stuff. Where she could just *be*.

She considered all of the things she had been keeping busy with since Mrs. Tibbs's arrival—avoiding Wiley and learning the Rules of Contact and everything else. Suddenly, Dahlia knew the real reason why she hadn't insisted they start searching for her Anchor: deep down, she hadn't really wanted to find it. Oh, she wanted to leave the manor all right. But maybe she was also a little bit afraid. And all that stuff about her past that she couldn't remember . . . what if some things were better forgotten?

But now everything had changed. Losing her cubby was like a big splash of cold water in her face. The more Dahlia sat on her tree, sinking slowly down into the trunk, looking back at the house with glazed eyes, the more she knew she was ready to start. Right now. She wasn't going to wait another second.

She looked down at her feet, dangling in the air forty feet above the ground. The patent-leather shoe on her right foot was big and chunky alongside the dainty bare toes of her left foot. Enough with letting things drag her down. Dahlia kicked hard, wiggled and shook until her shoe tumbled right off. It hung in the air for a second, an expired object loosed from its owner, almost like it couldn't believe its luck at being so unexpectedly freed. With a little quiver, the shoe flipped over in a gust of wind and started to drift up. *Always rising*, Dahlia thought as she watched the shoe pick up speed, surfing the gusts of wind, passing through the Boundary without even a moment's pause. A smile pulled at her lips.

The shoe was gone. And soon, Dahlia would be too.

Across the yard, Mrs. Tibbs shimmered through the front wall of the house. She wore a concerned frown, but Dahlia waved to show her that all was well and she had regained her gumption.

"Rank Wiley," she muttered to herself. "You've messed with the wrong ghost." She raised her voice and called, "Mrs. Tibbs— let's get to work! I want to find my Anchor and I want to find it fast. Today, if we can. Then that pawky man will get up tomorrow and find his Spectrometer sitting on a big fat zero."

Chapter 12

Back in the sunroom, Oliver was still reeling over what he had seen. What *had* he seen? A ghost . . . and a ghost-*room* . . . and then . . . then suddenly it was gone, all gone. Rank Wiley had been true to his word, Aspirating that amazing structure right down to the last molecule, where it lay twitching and bulging inside his now puffed-out backpack.

This was clearly the high moment of Wiley's whole life. He preened and strutted around the room, twisting his head from side to side as if facing a chorus of cheers and applause. "No need for thanks—no need for thanks," he said. "I'm Rank T. Wiley of Ghostermintors, Inc. It's what I do. All in a day's work, all in a day's work."

Oliver shuddered. The man was actually *proud* of what he'd done. And . . . a wave of shame washed over Oliver. He had actually *helped* the ghosterminator do it!

Wiley rubbed his hands together, then reached back and

patted his Aspirator as if it were an affectionate dog. "My machine is quite full up now, wouldn't you know. I'll just zip back to my room and transfer the . . . *matter* to its storage chamber, free up some more space, hmmm? Then I'll be back on the job as quick as a blink. No rest for the hardworking ghosterminator, you can be sure of that! Not until I see every last specter safely stowed in the belly of my Aspirator."

It came to Oliver that his delay in talking to his parents was what had allowed this to happen. He had wanted to stay in this house—he *still* wanted to, more than anything else in the world; if he were honest, even more now than before, considering it came with its very own ghost. Or it used to. But he'd let his own wants blind him to what had to be done.

"So," said Wiley, pulling both his arms up above his head in a full-body stretch, "I suppose it's time to unfold the rest of my plan, yes? A fine coup this morning—a very fine coup. You can see that we've completely demolished the creature's lair. But it's plain that we have not yet reached the *root* of the infestation. We have not yet found *the ghost itself!*"

Oliver's eyes widened. The ghost! That girl he'd seen—it must be her. He remembered the look on her face—this was no monster, no *creature*. This was a real person . . . only, well, see-through. And not alive. But she had looked sad and hurt and angry that her home was being destroyed. And why shouldn't she?

"Why do you have to do this stuff?" he yelled suddenly, startling Wiley so much that his Spectrometer fell to the floor with a clatter. "Why do you have to chase after harmless creatures? What did they ever do to you?"

Wiley frowned. "Hmmm," he said. "Well, perhaps I was mistaken. I had reckoned you for a kindred spirit, a fellow scientific mind. I see now that I have been wrong about you." He marched forward and yanked the goggles off Oliver's face. "*Completely* wrong. And now . . ." He spun around, nose in the air, and marched toward the sunroom door. "I have things to do. Getting ready for my groundbreaking scientific discoveries is something of a full-time job, as it turns out. La di da, young Oliver." And he swept out.

Good riddance! Oliver thought. The room seemed to relax with Wiley's departure, but it also seemed sad and somehow empty. Nothing had changed—at least, nothing that Oliver could see. But it was different nonetheless; something intangible was gone, and the hole it left ached like a phantom limb.

Oliver sighed and started down the hall. He had to make things right and fast, before Wiley did any more damage. He would tell his parents the whole story. They would send Wiley packing and Silverton Manor would be a much safer place.

He was halfway to the kitchen when he heard a gong echo through the house, followed by the patter of feet hurrying from the opposite direction. The front door! Oliver quickened his pace, wondering who it could be.

Mom got there before he did, but only just. He came

up behind her as she opened the heavy front door. "Good morning, Mr. Rutabartle," Mom said. She held in one hand a measuring tape that stretched down the hall behind her. A streak of dust smudged her forehead and a cobwebby feather duster stuck out of her messy bun. "How . . . nice to see you again. Please, come in."

She didn't sound like she especially wanted him to come in; she actually sounded like she wanted to get right back to her Party Zombie tasks, but Rutabartle did not seem at all put off. "No need for that, Mrs. Day," he said. "I've got an appointment back at the office on the half-hour. I just stopped by to deliver this." He put a crisp white envelope into her hand. He raised his sunglasses, looking up and down the hallway. "Is everything well? All looking good in here?"

"Oh, sure," said Mom distractedly. Her fingers were tip-tapping all over the envelope, like she wanted to start filling all that white space with to-do lists. "By the way, thank you for sending your fix-it man over so promptly. He's gotten right to work."

"Fix-it man?" said Rutabartle. "But I didn't . . . Ah! Greta—my new secretary!—she's a gem. She must be even more on the ball than I'd thought. Excellent; I'm glad you're taken care of." He took a step back, sliding his sunglasses into place like a parenthesis closing his visit.

"Oh, not so quickly!" Mom said, moving a step closer. There was a scuffling sound as Mom ripped the back side off the envelope Rutabartle had given her. Oliver smirked. She hadn't been tapping her fingers at all—she actually *had* been making a list. "This will get us started," she said.

Oliver craned his neck and could just make out the top lines: *gravel for the front walkway*; *new topsoil for the flower-beds*; *decorative bushes?*; *rust removal expert for the front gate* . . . The list was surprisingly long for the ninety seconds or so she'd spent writing. But then again, this was Party Zombie Mom they were dealing with, and Rutabartle was no match for her mad skills.

His eyes widened as he took in the list. "This is quite . . . er, do you really think all this . . . ?"

"Do you want to sell this house?" Mom's tone was frosty.

Rutabartle inclined his head, as though this wasn't a battle he wanted to fight. "Very well. I'll put Greta right on this. You can expect them to begin arriving first thing tomorrow morning." He turned away quickly, but Party Zombie Mom had one last parting shot.

"Those mover fellows who came with our stuff," she said. "One was particularly helpful—Beano, I believe his name was? Send him over as well. Our fix-it man is extraordinarily elusive. Not that there isn't enough to do around this place! But I could use a hand with some of the smaller chores."

Jock Rutabartle fled down the steps, waving a token good-bye over his shoulder. It was a good thing for him too, Oliver thought with a grin, because as his car door slammed and the engine started up, Mom was yelling, "Oh, wait! One more thing!"

The engine squealed and Rutabartle shot out of the driveway.

Mom sighed. "Never mind, we can make do for now, I suppose." She turned and focused her laser gaze on Oliver. "Aha," she said, and Oliver's heart sank. She had that look in her eye.

"Mom," he said quickly. "There's something really important I need to tell you about that guy—"

But Mom had turned her attention to the letter Rutabartle had given her. She tossed aside what was left of its envelope and frowned over its contents. She looked back up at Oliver. "That Rutabartle's a strange one, isn't he? In any case, if we expect prompt service we'll have to give it in return as well. You can be in charge of making sure this checklist is filled out by the end of the day. Get Poppy's help on it if you like. And when that's done, I want you both to report back to me. There are plenty of tasks that need to be done. It's going to be the party of the century!" Her eyes glazed over again. "How magnificent it's going to be!"

"But Mom, I really—"

Mom wasn't listening. She thrust the paper at Oliver and whirled off down the hallway toward the kitchen, dusting as she went.

Oliver ground his teeth. Not only had he not gotten to tell

her about Wiley, now he was stuck with chores. With a groan, he unfolded the paper in his hand. He read the title—*what?*—he must have misread. But no, he read it again: NORMALCY QUESTIONNAIRE.

What on earth?

NORMALCY QUESTIONNAIRE

Name:_____

Address:_____

Assigned by: <u>Jock Rutabartle, Town Commissioner</u>

How many children reside in the household? _____
Describe each child's age, interests, and favorite pastimes.

_____

_____

How often do children in the household engage in the following "normal" activities?

    a. Hopscotch
    b. Tic-tac-toe
    c. Video games
    d. Legos or other construction toys
    e. Other: _____

There was more—quite a lot more, and Oliver pored over every idiotic line. He turned the page over. On the back was an additional note:

HELPFUL SUGGESTIONS

Looking for a way to add more "normal" to your life? Want to learn how to blend in with the crowd? Follow these easy action steps and you'll be cruising with the rest of the world in no time.

1. *Don't make eye contact.* Interacting with those around you is the surest way to risk standing out. Keeping your eyes cast down, hands by your sides, is a much better way to adopt a perfectly ordinary stance.
2. *Avoid sudden movements.* A slow, steady pace is the way to go! No dashing or jumping or jerking about. If you want to truly be . . .

Oliver couldn't stand to read another gag-worthy word. He fought the urge to rip the paper into shreds, dig a deep hole, and bury it where it would never be found. But Mom had asked him to fill it out, and there was no way she would listen to him about Wiley until then. He also *still* hadn't made any progress on figuring out how they were going to stay in the house.

He set off for the circular staircase. It was time for him and Poppy to regroup, take time answering some miserable questions, and maybe—if they were lucky—come up with some solutions that would magically solve all of their problems.

If only it could be that easy.

Chapter 13

Silverton Manor was enormous. Dahlia had always known this, and had spent years wafting around the various rooms to no particular purpose. But when it came to actually going through it for information, like a prospector panning for gold in one of those ancient television shows she'd used to watch with her mother—well, for the first time she understood how big it really was.

"We should begin on the ground floor," Dahlia said at last. "It's where my mother spent just about all her time. It's the most likely spot for us to find clues about my Anchor."

"I suppose," Mrs. Tibbs murmured, just as Mrs. Day burst down at the far end of the hall, a pile of bedding teetering in her arms.

It was clear that if they didn't get busy soon, any potential clues would be buried under the stampede of progress and reorganization. Dahlia and Mrs. Tibbs ghosted through the wooden door into the living room. Of the surfaces she passed through every day, wood was Dahlia's favorite. Plastic was so slight she hardly noticed it. Brick was a little rough and scratchy to her insides. But wood was spongy and velvety, and tickled every time she passed through it. Maybe because it had once been alive, like her.

After all that, though, investigating the first floor went remarkably quickly. The guest room and mudroom had been fully taken over by Wiley's paraphernalia, which Dahlia found utterly distasteful. And she hated to go into the sunroom now, for being reminded of her lost cubby. Despite all this, over their next days of searching they quickly saw that the downstairs held no surprises. Dahlia had spent most of her time ghosting around on this floor, and knew every hidden nook and cranny. The kitchen might bear a closer look—there were several secret drawers and hidey holes that Dahlia knew of but had never bothered to examine in great detail, with their unexpired goods that she had never been able to handle—but the ghosts didn't dare poke around there while the living folks were zipping in and out. They resolved to come back under cover of darkness, when the house was quiet and the Day family asleep.

On the second floor Mr. and Mrs. Day had settled into the master bedroom, and the twins into a room across the hall. There was also a bathroom, a laundry room, and an endlessly long hallway that looked down over the huge living room and ended in a curved staircase leading to the front foyer. To Dahlia, everything appeared just as it always had—with the exception of all the newly moved-into areas, and she had to admit that most of the setup and decor was a huge improvement.

But as hard as both she and Mrs. Tibbs looked, there was not a leading clue nor a meaningful scrap of paper to be found.

Then they entered the library. Dahlia had never been much of a reader when she was alive—that she remembered, anyway—but there was nothing like being dead for fifty-eight years to give you an appetite for literature. Many times over her ghostly years she'd eyed those volumes, lined up all unread and tempting. Every time she'd tried to pick one up, her hands had shot right through its unexpired covers. But now . . . the idea that with a little more practice she might be able to pick up any book off the shelf and simply start to read was thrilling.

Dahlia gave herself a little shake. She wasn't here to read; she was here for action. Still, where to begin looking? Three wide walls were lined with floor-to-ceiling bookshelves, and heavy curtains closed off the fourth wall. The whole room was dim and dull and dingy.

"How are we going to search this place for clues?" she asked despairingly. It seemed so vast!

Mrs. Tibbs drifted across the plush carpet, which was coated in a thick layer of dust. Clearly Mrs. Day had not yet made her way into this room, though several boxes labeled

BOOKS were stacked just outside the door. Scooting toward the curtained wall, Dahlia drew up alongside the heavy velvet window drapes and started tugging. It took her four or five tries, and more than one accidental plunge through the wall into the outside, but finally she made Contact and managed to pull one of the curtains open a few inches. A fat beam of sunlight slid in from outside and set the dust motes sparkling.

Mrs. Tibbs turned from where she had been examining a bookshelf, and lifted her eyebrows. "Are you seeking illumination, my glum gollywog?"

Dahlia kept tugging. "A little light, yes. It's awfully gloomy in here! I've always hated these curtained-in rooms. And nighttime too, all that darkness everywhere. I don't like it one bit. I know I'm a ghost and I don't need to sleep, but you know, most nights I would just curl up on my own recliner and go to sleep till morning!" That made Dahlia think of her cubby, which made her start to feel soggy inside, but all of that skipped right out of her mind when she suddenly noticed . . . "Why, Mrs. Tibbs! You're glowing!"

The Liberator had drifted away from the books and now hovered in front of an ornate standing lamp, and at first Dahlia thought the lamp had been turned on. But no: a gentle core of light was gathering inside Mrs. Tibbs, growing and filling her all the way up in bright white light.

"Mrs. Tibbs," Dahlia breathed. "You're like some kind of star! It's so beautiful! Can I . . . can I do that too?"

"Of course," said Mrs. Tibbs. "It's simply a matter of drawing on the hidden particles inside matter, and turning them around to display their unseen core."

"Uh . . ." Dahlia hadn't caught any of that.

"Here," said Mrs. Tibbs, grabbing Dahlia's hand in her own. It was warm as well as bright, and as their fingers connected, the yellow-white glow slid into Dahlia's hand and up her wrist. And she understood—she felt the particles of darkness all around her, saw the pinpricks of light at their core, and could see how to tease out the buried strains of light, pulling them all the way inside her until she too was glowing like a miniature furnace.

"I want to rocket through the sky like a shooting star!" she crowed. "But not right now. Thank you for teaching me this, Mrs. Tibbs—it's positively amazing." In the light of their two glowing bodies, Dahlia turned all the way around and surveyed the library, sweeping her eyes over the shelves. Could there be something in here? Some clue to her past?

She hadn't spent much time in this room as a ghost, and her memories from early childhood didn't fit here at all. But something about the room still felt somehow familiar. Closing her eyes, Dahlia let her body tell her where to move, let herself drift back to a time when she had been floor-bound and needed to walk to get anywhere. She swept across the floor and when she opened her eyes she was standing in front of a small, friendly-looking bookshelf. Dusty, faded volumes cluttered the low shelf, and Dahlia's eyes passed over the titles: *Jack and Jill. Pippi Longstocking. Betsy and Tacy Go Downtown.* She used to read these. These were her books. This was her shelf.

She crouched down and ran her fingers over the spines, but after the first thrill of excitement, she felt nothing. There were no tingles, no tug of energy. Not even a nasty-smell feeling, like she'd felt from that closed-up attic room. Nothing. Just dead pages, bits of her old life that had been left here to fall apart in dust and ruin.

Dahlia gathered herself up. "Let's go."

But Mrs. Tibbs was on the other side of the room, drifting in a zigzag pattern along the far bookshelf wall. "Quite an interesting selection," she observed. She waved energetically. "This whole wall here—nothing but medical books! Every topic you can imagine, but a good deal on depression, dementia, mental illness, and so on. I have to say, it's quite unusual to find such a dense collection in an average person's home. Perhaps there was a doctor in the family?"

Dahlia frowned. "I don't think so. My mother wasn't, anyway. And I don't think my father—I don't think—" Something jarred her. Her father? She had hardly thought of him for decades, though she wasn't exactly certain why. Now that it came to it, she could remember next to nothing about him. Just a flash of beard, light curly hair ... and nothing else. Except—"He was not a doctor." She knew that positively. "He did something with cars, or travel. That's all I can remember."

Mrs. Tibbs turned away, and Dahlia sighed. "I'm afraid this is another dead end." She moved toward the door, and then let out a little cry. There on a small coffee table was a huge, black-leather-covered volume. It lay open with a thin red ribbon marking the page. Opaque dust lay heavily over the surface, but not nearly so much dust as Dahlia had seen on the far side of the room. This table and chair and this book had seen regular use—not recent, but not too long ago, either.

"She used to sit here sometimes and read. It's a Bible," Dahlia said slowly, remembering. Then her eyes lit up. "A *family* Bible! I heard her say so. I know this." Concentrating hard, she brushed a layer of dust off the open pages. The dust was light and came off easily, gusting up into the air and glinting in her body's glow like a cloud of late-afternoon fireflies. But try as Dahlia might, she couldn't get the pages to turn. They were stiff and crinkly and settled in place, and the combined effort of trying to make Contact while not ripping them clear out of the book tied her hands up in knots. Finally she groaned in frustration and flopped over onto the nearby armchair. And fell through it to the floor.

By the time she'd picked herself out of the upholstery, Mrs. Tibbs had flipped the book open to its title page. Dahlia came to hang over Mrs. Tibbs's shoulder as the older ghost turned several pages, coming at last to a carefully written family tree. It began in the mid-eighteen hundreds with Archibald Silverton, who married Margaret Lawrence. They had one daughter, Laura, who died in her teens, and two sons, both of whom married and carried on the Silverton name. The younger son had a daughter and died in middle age, along with his wife.

The elder son, Archibald Silverton, Jr., had two daughters and, very late in life, a young son.

The lists went on like this for a number of pages until the very last one, which bore only the words:

Reginald Silverton + Ernestine Clemments
Dahlia Silverton

None of these three names bore any dates—neither for birth nor death. But the ink on Dahlia's name was wavery, as though several small wet drops had splashed on it shortly after it was written. As though someone had sat in this very chair, perhaps, aching for a daughter who was no more.

"But I'm still here," Dahlia whispered, and something inside tightened into a knot and squeezed. "I'm still here, and where have all the rest of you gone?" She stayed motionless for a few minutes, head lowered, chest heaving, until she felt a warm touch on her shoulders. She tilted her head and leaned in to Mrs. Tibbs's hug. Then she lifted her shoulders in determination. "Let's go," she said quietly. "There's nothing more to see here."

✳

They were silent as they drifted up through the ceiling and emerged on the third floor. The thud of feet announced the Day family stampeding down for dinner—which, based on the tiny smell-bubbles expiring through the air, seemed like an especially fragrant beef stew—and the two ghosts emerged in the portrait room. Except . . . it was a little different from the last time Dahlia had been here.

"Oh, my lucky stars!" she exclaimed. The heirloom paintings still lined the walls, but all the end tables and decorative knickknacks had been pushed to one end. The other end was entirely filled by a giant blue-and-green-striped circus tent. It was half-collapsed but easily large enough, once assembled, to comfortably fit several adults. Crates of equipment and boxes of machinery cluttered the floor, and scattered here and there— actually placed in neat piles all along the center of the floor, Dahlia now saw—were dozens of small, hand-sized puppets. Circus performers. Of course. She'd seen Mr. Day hard at work, but hadn't realized this was the room he'd taken over. Nor that he had done it so completely. And colorfully.

"At least he's left the walls untouched," Dahlia said, turning away from the colorful wreckage and waving her hand at the peevish-looking faces that lined the walls. "Well, here you have my relatives! Some of them, anyway." There were twelve portraits down one side, eleven down the other, and the original Lord and Lady Silverton in a gilded place of honor at the non-circus end. Her mother's portrait was especially lovely, with Ernestine Silverton looking about eighteen years old and glowing with apple-cheeked health and beauty. For the first time it occurred to Dahlia to wonder why there was no portrait of her father in this room. Or of her, for that matter.

And at that moment she registered something she hadn't ever noticed before.

"Right here," she whispered. There was one blank spot on the side of the wall that held just eleven portraits—one perfectly canvas-sized blank spot. The kind of place where a painting might have once hung and been removed, with nothing left in its place. "An empty spot, just like me." Her eyes filled with tears, but she knew she couldn't handle another moment like the one she'd just had in the library. She squeezed her hands tightly, focusing all her energy on tamping down her emotion. She *would not cry*.

Under her foot, something squeaked.

Dahlia jumped. An evil little pink puppet face stared up at her, grinning a manic red-painted grin. Dahlia leaped three feet and fell halfway into a nearby portrait before she collected herself and let out a low groan. "The Days are taking over this house, Mrs. Tibbs, and all I've got to show for my clues are lists of names and a blank spot for a painting. Sometimes I think I'm going to be stuck in this house for good. Or until old Wiley gets me, anyway." She wasn't usually so gloomy, but to search all day and find practically nothing—nothing but sad, lonely spots, and tear-stained family trees—made her feel lower than a fruit fly.

Just then, there was a scuffle at the door. "Speak of the devil," muttered Mrs. Tibbs as Wiley burst in, nose aquiver, eyes darting from side to side.

"Come on, my pretties," he crooned, like the ghosts might be lured over to him by the sweetness of his song.

Dahlia narrowed her eyes as her emotions did a quick *zing*, sharpening from sadness to white-hot anger to a deep sense of determination. Fruit fly, huh? Well, she still had some buzz left in her. "Let's skedaddle," she said. "Maybe there's something to find in this old house and maybe there isn't, but I'm not going to give myself up to this joker."

And with that she zipped off, Mrs. Tibbs trailing in her wake.

Chapter 14

In the few days since the sunroom incident, Oliver had been puzzling over what to do about Rank Wiley. With Poppy's grudging help, Oliver had filled out the stupid Normalcy Questionnaire. There was nothing too strange on there—well, aside from the fact that a Normalcy Questionnaire even *existed*—but it came down to this: Mr. Rutabartle really, *really* wanted everything in Silverton Manor to be "normal." He wanted the flowerbeds to look like normal flowerbeds. He wanted the children to run and skip and play like normal children. *Good luck with that*, Oliver thought, watching Joe and Junie zip past wearing giant brightly decorated paper bags, singing a nursery rhyme in pig latin.

Once the questionnaire was out of the way, Oliver had tried to corner his parents about Wiley, but they had proved even more resistant than expected. He'd managed to separate Mom from her to-do list three separate times, but each attempted explanation left him feeling more foolish than the last. Mom's reactions went from long-suffering patience to exasperation to curt dismissal. Yesterday he'd finally managed to drag her over to confront Wiley, and had found the man taking apart a pipe in the downstairs bathroom.

"Making very good headway here, as you can see," he'd stammered out with a big cheesy grin upon seeing Mom.

Oliver knew there had to be more to it—Wiley's Spectrometer was right there on the floor next to him. But Mom had just rolled her eyes and started listing online stores that sold coordinating bathroom sets. And Oliver had realized that he was on his own.

So now he was back to the original plan: shadow the ghosterminator, suss out all his cameras and whatever other secrets he might be hiding, and then figure out how to upset his evil shenanigans and send him running.

Or something like that.

Oliver peered around the corner and up the stairs. Above him, a board squeaked as Wiley moved along the upper landing. Oliver skidded out from his hiding spot and shot up the stairs on the ghosterminator's trail. He heard the opening of a door, and footsteps—and quite suddenly, his mother's voice, loud and businesslike.

"There you are again, Mr. Wiley. How are things coming along today with the maintenance and updates?"

Oliver ducked into an alcove and leaned one eye around the edge to see what was going on. Wiley stood halfway into the portrait room, his arms full of ghosterminating equipment shoved guiltily behind him. Mom had her hands on her hips.

"Erm, yes," Wiley said, a little too quickly but then making a good recovery. "The downstairs bathroom is just as good as new. For the rest, I've been working on, er, compiling a full assessment. I expect I'll soon have to make a trip into town to collect some materials—and, yes, this room seems already to be well taken care of. Overall, things are shaping up."

Mom narrowed her eyes, and Oliver's heart leaped. At last! She was going to see Wiley was a useless junk collector and kick him right down the front steps. But then Mom seemed to relax. "Good, I'm glad to hear it. For now, though, I want you to set aside the assessment work. I've already got workers tending to the outside of the house. Mr. Rutabartle left specific instructions. I believe you said something about heating systems when you first arrived?"

"Uh, certainly . . ."

"Excellent. That's what you should tend to next, then. Last night the temperature dropped below forty degrees, and the insulation on this place is practically nonexistent. We've got space heaters running in every room, but I don't want to keep using those all winter. Will you conduct a full inspection of all the vents and the boiler, and make sure that all is as it should be before we turn the heat on? It probably hasn't been used in years."

Wiley cleared his throat. "Of course, Mrs. Day. I can do

that. In fact, I will begin this very instant." With that, he spun around, somehow managing to keep his Spectrometer and other tools out of Mom's view, scooted past the alcove—catching Oliver's eye with an annoyed scowl—and slunk down the stairs toward his guest room.

Oliver leaned farther back out of sight, but thankfully Mom marched off in the other direction. Just when he thought he was safe, a voice hissed in his ear: "What are you doing in there?"

"Hey!" Oliver yelped, coming out of the shadows with a frown for Poppy. "Are you sneaking around behind me? I told you not to do that!"

Poppy shrugged and fell into step beside him as they walked down the hallway. "I'm bored. My room's all set up and nothing else is going on."

"Don't let Mom hear you say that. Or better yet, *do* let her and you'll be out of my way for a good long time."

"I know you're up to something. Why won't you tell me what it is?"

"I'm not up to anything," Oliver said with a groan.

"I helped you with that questionnaire when I didn't have to. You owe me."

Oliver thought fast. "Listen, what I'm really doing is trying to find a way for us to keep this house. *Remember?*" He felt bad saying this, because Wiley and the questionnaire had so occupied his time recently that he actually *hadn't* been putting any time into that side of things. He quickly added, "We really need to think of how we can talk Mom and Dad into it."

A door opened right in front of them and Dad emerged, blinking like a mole coming out of its burrow. "Talk Mom and Dad into what, exactly?"

Oliver froze. He hadn't expected to make his argument so soon, but . . . "This place, Dad," he said. "This house. Isn't it amazing? We keep moving—how many houses have we been to in the last five years? And don't even get me started on all the new schools."

Poppy kicked him, but it was too late. Dad reached up to stroke his chin. "Schools! Yes, that's right—we got a call from the vice principal of Longwood Elementary and Middle School a few days ago, and I've been meaning to call her back. You still have the packets from your correspondence course, but it might be good for you to finish out the year in town, don't you think?"

"Dad!" Oliver said, exasperated. This wasn't how he'd imagined the conversation going. "I don't want to talk about going to school. Don't you get how awful moving is, how much we hate it? We need a *home*, somewhere to belong. And we think the best place to stay is right here!"

Dad thought about this. Then he sighed and straightened the brim of his hat. "I don't know what to tell you, son," he said, beckoning Poppy over to his other side and putting an arm around each of them. "This is our job, house caretaking.

Of course it was all fun and games when we started out. I'm the first to admit that over the past couple years, it's gotten more challenging . . . but it's what we do! And I know it always seems like prosperity is right around the corner, that *big success* that will let us settle down somewhere. But now with The Jolly Marzipans starting to take off . . . well, who knows? I think they might be the one!"

"Dad, you always think your newest troupe is going to be the one," Poppy said gently.

"But you haven't seen this show yet! It's like nothing that's ever been done before. My lucky hat is humming! Once the show is up, we'll have many more options. In fact, I was thinking we could do a live demonstration for your mother's Halloween party. Wouldn't that be a nice touch?"

"So you think," said Oliver, steering Dad back onto the subject, "that if this show does well, and if we have enough money in April—for a good down payment, at least—maybe we could buy this place?"

"We'll just have to see," said Dad. Which was better than *no*, if just barely.

Poppy rolled her eyes, shrugging out of Dad's grasp and scooting over next to Oliver. "Like that's going to happen," she whispered. "Didn't you hear Rutabartle? He's going to *auction* it off. A house like this has to be worth tons of money."

"I don't know," Oliver said thoughtfully. Dad kept walking, probably lost in some circus dream, but Oliver pulled on Poppy's ruffled sweatshirt, dragging her off to the side. "What about all that talk of curses in the village? People are scared of this place. And think of how the grounds look, and all the work the house needs, even on the inside. Plus, we're out in the middle of nowhere. Literally. How much could a place like this go for?"

"More than Mom and Dad will ever have in their bank account," said Poppy shortly. With that she straightened her sweatshirt and marched off after Dad.

Oliver frowned. He knew Poppy was right, and yet . . . he couldn't let go of the idea. The house had crawled inside his head—he would have said his heart, even, except that was just weird—and whatever it took, he had to find some way for them to keep it. "My coin collection!" he said suddenly. He had a huge monster jar of coins that he'd been saving up since his eighth birthday. Obviously there wouldn't be enough in there to buy a house, but . . . it would be a start. He'd count that up, and then start figuring out how to save as much as possible, as quickly as possible.

Six months wasn't very long, but it would have to be long enough. His future at Silverton Manor depended on it.

Chapter 15

The rest of the third floor was a bust: Dahlia and Mrs. Tibbs found nothing—not a single scrap of paper, suspicious prickling object, or even anything interesting to look at. The third floor had obviously not been used in many years and, with the exception of the portrait-turned-puppet room, nowhere else appeared to have been touched by the Days either.

It was late into the night by the time they made it up to the attic. Dahlia was all ready to practice her new glowing skills, but Mrs. Tibbs explained that Lightening, as it was called, drew a lot of ghostly power. With Wiley sticking his Spectrometer in every nook and cranny, they had to be very careful. So they stayed dark while moving through the house and always used Clearsight to make sure the ghosterminator was away from his instruments before they switched themselves on (as Dahlia liked to imagine it).

Now Wiley was sound asleep in his bed, as were all the

members of the Day family, and the various gutter cleaners, landscapers, and random repairmen had long since left for the night. The house felt nearly as empty and quiet as it had been before the Days moved in. Now that she was getting the hang of this Contact business, Dahlia had a crazy desire to find a random floorboard to squeak, the better to feel like a real ghost. But she restrained herself and floated along next to Mrs. Tibbs as they made their way up toward the attic. They could have just gone straight through the floors to reach the top, but Dahlia liked following the twists and turns of the hallway. It felt comforting somehow, especially since they were looking for clues from before she'd died.

On the last flight of stairs Mrs. Tibbs crossed her feet at the ankles, folded her hands in her lap, and slid up the banister. Dahlia laughed so hard that a ribbon on her dress came loose and started drifting upward. She yanked on it and smushed it back into place.

But in spite of these moments of lightness, Dahlia couldn't help but worry. They had searched almost the whole house. What if her Anchor couldn't be found?

"So here we have the attic," Mrs. Tibbs mused as they came up through the wide opening. To the left of the stairs was a garish yellow-and-orange-checkered wall. It was, in fact, the only wallpapered surface; the rest of the landing area had been slapped with an uneven coat of sky-blue paint. This wall seemed excessive for some reason Dahlia couldn't figure out, and even more strange—when she tried focusing her Clearsight, she couldn't see through it at all. With a jolt she realized that this was the dull, smudgy part of the house that looked so rotten when she'd scanned the house that first day.

"Can you see through that wall, Mrs. Tibbs?" she asked, and when the other ghost shook her head, looking just as puzzled as she felt, Dahlia continued, "It's almost like one of those black boxes downstairs, the ironite you told me about." She ran her hand along its surface. The wall seemed to be charged with some kind of electrical energy, and no sooner did she move away than a low rumble shook the floor around them. Dahlia jumped back. "What *is* this place?"

"Most peculiar," said Mrs. Tibbs. "It does appear that a barrier has been erected, but not by a living person. This is ghost-driven."

"Maybe that's where my Anchor is," Dahlia exclaimed. "We haven't found anything in the house—it must be in here!"

But Mrs. Tibbs was shaking her head. "I don't think so, dearie. Your Anchor wouldn't just board itself up all on its own. It's an inanimate object, you know. Much more likely the interference derives from a buildup of ghostly energy—we might need to call an Investigator if it doesn't resolve itself before too long. It feels rather old, as well. Has this blockage always been here?"

The truth was, Dahlia didn't know. It sounded silly to say that she hadn't noticed the bad spot before, but she had been so busy avoiding the upper floors that she hadn't paid them close enough attention. And even now, it was almost as though she didn't *want* to delve deeper into this area, like the energy in the room was pushing her away. If she hadn't been on a specific mission, she wondered if she would have recognized it even now.

It was just as well that her Anchor wasn't in there, since there was no way inside. There was still a great deal of attic to explore, and where could be better to hide treasures? To the right of the landing was a closed door, which led to a tiny finished bedroom. Oliver lay inside, sprawled on his bed fully dressed and sound asleep. Behind his room opened a much wider space, which filled the whole rest of the upper area of the house—the real, bonafide storage portion of the attic. Dahlia rubbed her hands together gleefully: a veritable junkyard. They would hit the jackpot here for sure!

Dahlia activated her Lightening the moment they passed into the storage area. Light flooded the room. She smiled. "I can't tell you how good it feels to be able to do that. All those nights I spent in darkness—I can hardly imagine it now! I'm a girl-shaped lightning bug."

Mrs. Tibbs chuckled. "Tut-tut, my dear. You're a good deal more than that!"

The storage area was jammed full of boxes, twenty or thirty or more crowded into the small space. A row of clothes on hangers cut across the far corner: fur jackets and out-of-date suit coats and lacy, old-fashioned dresses. Two long, low shelves held dozens of pairs of shoes. An assortment of parcels and packages filled the last corner.

There was no telling what might be important, so they began in opposite corners. Mrs. Tibbs started moving among the clutter, lifting boxes and opening the flaps, peering at the contents, leafing through books and papers, reading scraps and humming tunelessly all the while. Dahlia, no matter how hard she tried, still couldn't lift anything heavier than a piece of cloth, so she settled for ghosting through things. Beginning with the stack nearest to her, she ran her hand through each object, paying attention for any special prickles that might indicate buried memories or any type of connection. There would be a certain energy, Mrs. Tibbs had told her, making it plain when an object was connected to her Anchor.

"Mrs. Tibbs," Dahlia said, as she swept her hand through a rusty tin of marbles, biting back a giggle at the gritty chill of so many tiny glass balls passing through her hand. "I've been meaning to ask you—how did you become a Liberator?"

Mrs. Tibbs gave Dahlia a broad smile. Pausing in her search to reach into her carpetbag, the older ghost pulled out an ornate pocket watch on a long gold chain. The outer case was etched in small swirls, and it looked half-transparent.

Dahlia's mouth dropped open. "That watch is not expired, is it?"

Mrs. Tibbs shook her head. "This belonged to my poor dear Charley. My other half. He's still alive, I'm sorry to say. Oh, child, I missed him so much the first few years after I crossed over. For a while I hung around him just because. But the Ghouncil finally got me going—they don't appreciate deviations, and they threatened me with all kinds of . . . well, enough of that. Suffice it to say that it was time for me to go, but before I did, I took his watch. Something to remember him by, and it was so dear to his heart. I hope he doesn't miss it too much." She sighed. "But he'll get it back someday. And I don't mind saying I hope he hurries up."

"How long has it been?" Dahlia's voice was soft.

"Twenty-one years next month," Mrs. Tibbs said. "But don't let me look like I'm complaining! I'm keeping busy while I wait."

"So you took up being a Liberator."

Mrs. Tibbs nodded. "At first I thought I might be able to hang around Charley, but it doesn't work that way. I have been able to stop by every so often, between assignments. It keeps me on this side of the Divide and more importantly it keeps me busy. Keeps my mind off missing him. And"—she smiled—"as a bonus, I've gotten to meet some quite excellent ghosts in the process." She leaned back against a large square package. Dropping the watch back into her bag, she stretched her arms up over her head. "Come along then, my glimmering gosling. Let us keep calm and carry on, as they say." And she turned her attention to the box nearest her.

It wasn't long, though, before searching the attic began to get just as wearying as going through the rest of the house. Dahlia noticed the boxes were topped with neat white labels, which should have made things easier to search, but actually just showed them more quickly how useless all this junk was: WEDDING GARMENTS. DECORATIONS. FINE GLASSWARE. Nothing looked even remotely mysterious nor historical. Two of the boxes were marked PAPERS, ASSORTED. But this potentially hot lead chilled right out when the box ended up being full of childish artwork, receipts, and school report cards from a century ago. Fascinating for a local historian, no doubt, but quite useless for their search.

"And we still don't even know what we're looking for!" Dahlia said with a groan, dropping onto, then immediately tumbling through the dusty floor, using all her focus to try not to slip in further than her waist. "No wonder we haven't been able to find it."

Mrs. Tibbs finished her box and picked through every pocket of the hung-up clothes, turning up an array of coins, three wrapped gum sticks, and an old thimble. "Nothing worthwhile here," she said with a grunt.

Next she turned to the large square package she had leaned against earlier, unwrapping it to show a carefully preserved oil painting of a small girl wearing a pink frilly dress. Dahlia had passed her hand through the wrapping, to no particular sparkles. But now her eyes widened as Mrs. Tibbs held it up. "The missing spot in the portrait gallery!" she said. And then her hand flew up to cover her mouth. "Oh, Mrs. Tibbs—do you think . . . could that be . . . *me*?"

"I should say so." Mrs. Tibbs ran a ghostly finger lovingly over the rounded cheeks, the apple-green eyes, the reddish-gold curls. "What are you doing up here, dearie?" she crooned.

Dahlia's eyes filled with tears. "I don't understand," she whispered. "We've searched the whole house and I feel more in the dark than ever." Her ghostly glow faded with the emotion of the moment. "What if there *aren't* any clues in the house? What if I never find my Anchor?"

Mrs. Tibbs shook her head as she lashed the bundle back together. "Keep heart, my gorgeous glowworm. Clues are pesky like that. Nine times out of ten they turn up when you are least expecting them."

And that was when Dahlia fell into the floor a little too far, and something zapped her backside like she'd sat on ten thousand volts of ghostly electricity. Dahlia let out a bloodcurdling shriek as the whole world around her went black.

Chapter 16

Oliver was awakened by something like a yell—a quick, high sound that cut off almost the second he opened his eyes and sat bolt upright in bed. Poppy! But where? He reached for the lamp on his nightstand, then scowled when he remembered that the Matchbox didn't yet have a lamp. Or a nightstand.

He stood up and felt his way through the pitch black to the door, whispering, "Poppy?" He stepped toward the light switch, which was, inexplicably, in the hall outside the room. As he did, something caught his eye: a red winking light, two or three steps into the unfinished portion of the attic. Another one of Wiley's cameras? He thought he'd found all of them, but that ghosterminator seemed to be growing more shady every day. Oliver's eyes were adjusting to the dimness; through the skylight on the roof he could see the round, fat moon.

A scuffling noise caught his ear, coming from further in the attic. And . . . there it was again. A girl's voice.

But it wasn't Poppy.

Keeping to the darker shadows at the edges of the walls, Oliver crept closer. And there, illuminated in the stark light of the moon, he saw a girl about his own age. She was wearing an old-fashioned, weirdly frilly dress and had long corkscrew curls that waved around her face as she gestured wildly. She was talking to . . . nobody?

"—something down there, I tell you! I blacked out for a second after it zapped me. I went right inside it. What is—" She paused, and tilted her head like she was listening. "Well, I'm sure I don't know!" She thrust her hand down toward the floorboards. Her hand cracked hard against the floor and she shrieked again. "It's not going through! Oh, Mrs. Tibbs, what is going on?"

There were a few more seconds of silence, while the girl alternately shook and nodded her head. Then she said, "Just your hand—right through there. Oh!" There was a sudden *zap* and, to Oliver's shock, a bony old woman dropped out of the air and thudded to the ground at the girl's feet. A hat fell off the woman's head, and a head of silver hair glinted in the moonlight.

Oliver swallowed hard. *What* was going on?

Suddenly he remembered the winking light that had led him out here. Oh, no! Wiley's camera. Oliver had no idea who these people were or what they were doing in his attic, but he knew he didn't want Wiley spying on them. Darting across the floor, Oliver swiped the camera, yanking the plug out of the wall and shoving it in his pocket.

"What was that sound?" asked the girl. Oliver ducked behind a pile of boxes, anxious to stay out of sight until he could figure out what was going on.

"My Clearsight isn't working," the old woman said grimly. "I've no idea what that machine is, but it certainly isn't the type of clue we were looking for."

"I think . . . ," said the girl, and her voice wobbled. "I think it's made us not be ghosts anymore. Oh, Mrs. Tibbs, do you think we might be living again?"

Oliver couldn't tell from her voice whether that would be a good thing or a bad thing. But . . . had she said *ghosts*? Oh! The girl—the ghost he had seen in the room with Wiley— could they really be one and the same? Suddenly, Oliver was very glad he had disconnected the camera.

So wait . . . now he actually, truly believed that ghosts were *real*?

Oliver thought he needed to sit down for a minute and take all of this in.

"Living again!" The old lady harrumphed. Mrs. Tibbs, the girl had called her. "I should think not. I believe we are dealing with an old-fashioned Manifestation machine. I've heard tell of these: they have the ability to render a spirit briefly corporeal.

For a time the spirit can be seen, and heard, and felt by the living—but at the price of their own ghostliness, as it were."

"So that's why I can't put my hand through the floor anymore." The girl suddenly jumped up and down in place, and the floorboards squeaked under her. "Oh, this is too good! You can't believe how long it's been since I could properly jiggle a board. Imagine trying to haunt this place with my lack of ghost skills! All I've had to work with were dust and wind, and making *whooshing* sounds through keyholes." She rolled her eyes. "Amateur hour. Though I guess it worked okay for the most part." And she shook her fist comically, as though at imaginary vandals.

Oliver smiled in spite of himself. These were the ghosts Wiley was so upset about? They seemed so . . . normal. Not to mention visible. He still didn't have a clue what was going on, but he was awfully glad he hadn't slept through the excitement.

"Hush now, my giggling gargoyle. We mustn't draw attention to ourselves—especially not now."

"I think this is right about the time we'd like some attention. What's that boy's name? —He seemed nice enough. His room is right through there—we could go have a nice chat with him. Maybe he could help us look for clues." They were talking about *him*, clearly! Oliver frowned. This was probably the right time for him to come out and say or do something. But *what?*

Mrs. Tibbs reached over and grabbed the girl's arms. "Now, Dahlia. I must remind you that when it comes to their codes and bylaws, the Ghouncil is extremely particular. And one of their principal laws and regulations is this: absolutely no Dialoguing with the living. None whatsoever. We spoke about Manifesting, which is also highly forbidden, and the two often go together. But Dialoguing is the worst and most highly punishable offense of all! —Well, second only to Liberating Without a License. In any case, *you must not make Contact!*"

"Well, I think that's silly."

"Silly is as silly does." The woman picked up her hat and jammed it back on her head. "All I can tell you is that you don't want to tangle with the Ghouncil. You have not had cause to experience their wrath, and—well, let's just make sure and keep it that way, all right?"

"Oh, Mrs. Tibbs—look at my hand!"

Oliver noticed it too. Whatever had happened to make the girl—Dahlia—visible was wearing off: her left arm had almost completely disappeared. It was now or never. Taking a deep breath, Oliver stood up and stepped slowly from his hiding place. "Wait!" he whispered urgently. "I didn't understand everything you just said, but I'm not going to hurt you. I'm Oliver, and . . ."

He stopped, because his speech was not having the right effect. Dahlia was swiveling her head wildly between him and Mrs. Tibbs, like she was trying to figure out what to do. The older ghost, on the other hand, lifted her chin and folded her arms. She spoke to the air above Oliver's head. "I realize that I am able to be seen at this present time, which is a most unfortunate happenstance. However, it is plain that I am not speaking with any living person, as I do not have authority to do so, and in no way would I ever go beyond the Ghouncil's demands."

"Mrs. Tibbs!" Dahlia wailed. She was now just a floating torso.

"Please, let me help," Oliver said, turning to face her since the older ghost was obviously a lost cause. "You mentioned clues—let me help! What can I do for you? There's something under the floorboards that made you visible, right? Want me to pull it out for you?"

Oliver scanned the floor, trying to figure out what had made this weird thing happen, but he couldn't find anything. And when he looked up, Dahlia was completely gone. All he saw was old Mrs. Tibbs's disapproving glare. "Now you look here," she huffed. "That is to say, if I were a young boy right now, I would leave this room immediately and go back to bed. Oh, good gracious! Look at my feet! This is a most distressing sensation . . ."

As Oliver watched, the woman and her hat slowly dissolved into thin air. It was like watching special effects on TV, except every minute of this was real. Oliver was beside himself. The second the last jaunty blue flower vanished from sight he dropped to the floor and started pawing at the boards. *What* had made the ghosts visible? Where could he find it?

But before he'd had a chance to do more than sketch a few lines in the dust at the point where the ghosts had been standing, he heard a sound that made his heart screech to a stop: the plod of feet coming up the attic. And not just any feet. Not the tippy-tap of Poppy stalking him; not the thud-thud of Dad going for a midnight snack; not the scurry-patter of Mom working off her insomnia with some late-night cleaning.

No. Only one person in this house had that distinctive, predatory *clomp*, and he was getting closer.

Rank Wiley was on his way.

Oliver leaped up and scooted away from where he'd been standing. How much had Wiley seen through that camera before Oliver had turned it off? How much did he know? "Shoo!" he whispered behind him, having no idea where the ghosts were but knowing they did *not* want to mess with Wiley on the warpath. "This guy is dangerous—he's trying to capture you. You have to leave now!"

The last words were hardly out of his mouth before Wiley's head appeared at the top of the stairs, looking crafty and ferret-like, his Spectrometer held out in front of him and the Aspirator strapped to his back.

"You!" he growled, narrowing his eyes at Oliver. "I might have suspected you were wrapped up in this."

"I live here," said Oliver icily. "And you're standing in front of my bedroom door."

Wiley sniffed. "And I suppose you haven't seen my spectral

camera anywhere? It just vanished into thin air after registering some oddly paranormal phenomena?"

Oliver was glad for the dark attic, as he knew he probably
looked completely guilty. But Wiley had already pushed past
him. The readout on his Spectrometer hummed and crackled.

"Wait a minute," Oliver said. "About this ghost thing—can
we talk about it? I'm not sure you really understand what—"

Wiley shook him off. "Aha!" he crowed. "I believe we've hit
the jackpot!"

Before Oliver could grasp what was going on, Wiley reached
a hand up to his shoulder strap and switched the Aspirator on.
He yanked the nozzle forward. It was just like the sunroom, but
this time, Oliver knew it would be so much worse. From the
noises the Spectrometer was making, and the manic red buzz
of the pilot light, he could tell the ghosts hadn't left yet. What
were they waiting for? Were they still disoriented from switch-
ing back to their see-through bodies?

He threw himself at Wiley, knocking the man to the ground
with a thud. Another, louder rumble echoed farther back in the
attic, but Oliver hardly noticed. A jet of phoam spewed out of
the Aspirator; Oliver had knocked Wiley off balance and the
horrible stuff shot back toward the door. But in another second
Wiley was back on his feet, shoving Oliver out of the way.

"More than twenty years I've been waiting for this moment,"
Wiley panted.

He lifted the nozzle, aimed, and sprayed.

Chapter 17

It all happened so quickly. Dahlia was still trying to get herself back into ghosting mode, still getting used to the fact that she had talked to a boy—a living, breathing *boy*! A boy named Oliver!—as well as trying to grasp Mrs. Tibbs's warnings about Dialoguing. What kind of creeps were these Ghouncil folks, anyway? She'd like to give them and their demented rulebook a piece of her mind! Then suddenly that ghosterminator was back and brandishing his ghastly machinery and shooting out a jet of that awful specter-goo and Oliver was trying to stop him but the man was up again and too fast and then—

Dahlia stared in horror as the phoam shot straight toward them. It slopped down over Mrs. Tibbs's flowery hat, her long lean body, her lumpy carpetbag. In two seconds flat it covered her from head to toe.

"No!" Dahlia yelled. Neither the boy nor the horrible man could hear her. Mrs. Tibbs could, though. Through the gunk

Dahlia could see the Liberator's lips form a single word: "GO!" But Dahlia couldn't go. Frozen in place, she watched Wiley rev up his machine. He flipped the switch to start the Aspirating process. Oliver launched himself at the ghosterminator again, but Wiley was ready for him this time, swinging the Spectrometer and clocking him on the head. Oliver toppled to the ground.

It just took Dahlia a split second to turn her eyes and follow Oliver's fall. But when she looked back at the main attic area, the air in front of the door was empty.

Mrs. Tibbs was gone.

"No," Dahlia said again, whispering this time. She felt as if she were cracking in two.

There was a suck and a gurgle and a satisfied burp from Wiley's machine. Looking craftily in both directions, the ghosterminator packed up his belongings, took one last look at Oliver lying sprawled on the ground, and crept away down the stairs.

The Aspirator sack pushed and bulged on Wiley's back, as though something inside wanted very badly to get out but could not do so, no matter how hard it tried.

Wiley disappeared down the staircase, and Dahlia sat staring after him, feeling tied into a hundred knots. And frozen. And squashed under a blanket of paralyzing inactivity. What could she *do*? She had to save Mrs. Tibbs, but how? If she went after him, Wiley would Aspirate her too. Oh why, *why* hadn't she moved more quickly, found some way to keep Mrs. Tibbs from being captured?

On the attic floor, Oliver groaned.

A few things fell into place in Dahlia's mind all at once. She couldn't get to Wiley. But Oliver could. And . . . there was that device buried under the floorboards. Of course!

Dahlia swept over to the spot and peered through the floorboards. She could see it clearly now—it was made of some kind of ornate metal. It looked a little like an old-fashioned cash register and on the top, in fancy calligraphy, was the word *Seesaw.* She thought of Mrs. Tibbs's warning about Manifesting and Dialoguing. But who were these Ghouncil people anyway? What had they ever done for her? It was a ridiculous notion, having a living boy right here and available to help but not being able to access him. For every rule there was an exception, right?

Gritting her teeth, Dahlia jammed her hand into the center of the machine. She was ready for the jolt this time, so it didn't throw her completely off balance, and while everything around her still went dark, she didn't lose consciousness. She hit the floor with a thump and took a second to orient herself. Then she jumped up and ran over to Oliver, who was pulling himself into a sitting position.

"Are you all right?" she said, putting a hand on his arm. To her amazement, she *could*!

"Oh!" Oliver goggled at her and she scooted back.

"I'm Dahlia Silverton," she said quickly. "Is your head okay? That creep clocked you good. And . . ." Her eyes got blurry. "He trapped my friend, Mrs. Tibbs, in one of his machines."

"I'm Oliver Day," he said. "I'm fine. He didn't hit me very hard—I think I just lost my balance."

"The thing is," Dahlia said, "I really need your help. We have to find a way to get Mrs. Tibbs back."

Oliver nodded. "I want to help, but I'm not sure I know how. That guy is sneaky and, well, basically horrible."

Dahlia looked at him. He looked back.

"I guess the first thing we need to do is get that machine up out of the floor," he said finally. "Don't you think?"

"The Seesaw," said Dahlia. "You're right. I saw a crowbar earlier when we were going through the attic." She walked awkwardly across the floor—she had forgotten how difficult it was to manage with living-person gravity. What a ridiculous way to get around! Figuring she didn't have too long—if her last experience was any indicator—she passed Oliver the crowbar and he dropped to his knees, prying at a board above the Seesaw's hiding spot.

"That ghosterminator will try to skedaddle out of here fast now that he's got what he came for," she said. "You have to stop him."

"Stop him from leaving? Are you joking? That's what he needs to do. I'm going to talk to my parents again first thing in the morning. I'll show them my lump and see if they still think I'm imagining things. He'll be on the road before breakfast is over!"

"No!" Dahlia grabbed his arm. "You can't! Don't you see? He'll *want* to leave now; he got what he came for. But if he leaves, *he takes Mrs. Tibbs with him*! I'll never see her again and she'll be trapped forever in that evil black box, and who knows what he'll do to her? He'll dissect her in the name of science and she'll never be with her Charley again!" A sob rose in her throat. She had to make him understand.

Oliver didn't seem to have a clue what she was talking about, but he passed his hand across his forehead. "So what do you want me to do?" He pried the crowbar alongside the other end of the board and kept working at it.

"Try to delay him for a little bit. Tell him . . . there's another ghost he needs to look for. That will keep him here."

"No!" said Oliver. "Then he'll go looking for you—and you definitely don't want that."

"Well then, something else. Make up some other ghost room," she swallowed, "like my cubby." An idea struck her. It was painful, but the only thing she could think of. "I have a garden outside. A real ghost garden. You can tell him about that—but don't tell him where it is until later. Only if you have to. See if you can keep delaying him, or tell him you need to look for the garden or something. More stuff for him to study. And meanwhile, we can find a way to free Mrs. Tibbs."

"The day after tomorrow is Mom's big Halloween bash—there's going to be all kinds of stuff going on, people coming in and out. Maybe we can find some way to break her out then."

Before Dahlia could reply, another voice cut through the quiet attic. "Hey, what's going on up here?"

Oliver let out a groan. "Poppy, not again," he said. "What are you doing out of bed? It's the middle of the night!"

"Well, *you're* not in bed, and I heard all this arguing going on up here. Did you know there's some kind of ventilation passage between here and the turret? Who knew, huh? Hey, who is *that*? Why is there a strange girl in our attic? OLIVER?!"

Oliver had dropped the crowbar and dashed across the attic floor to silence Poppy, putting both hands across her mouth. Poppy's eyes bulged.

"SHUSH!" Oliver whispered. "We don't want Mom or Dad to . . ."

Poppy shoved his hands off her face and started thrashing from side to side. "Mom and Dad are down on the second floor. They won't hear a thing. But you—need—to—get off me NOW!"

"Fine—as long as you HUSH!" Oliver let go and went back to his floorboard.

Eyes wide and shining, Poppy scuttled over to Dahlia. "So who *are* you? Wait, your legs—what happened to them? Are you going invisible?"

Oliver sighed. "Poppy, meet Dahlia. She's . . . um, a ghost. She lives in this house, and I only just met her."

"HAH!" Poppy called out, loud enough that Oliver clamped his hand back over her mouth. She shoved him away again. "Sorry—I'll be quiet. But didn't I tell you that there was *something* going on with this house? Am I EVER not right?"

Oliver rolled his eyes. "You thought there was something creepy-weird about this house, not cool-weird."

"Close enough," said Poppy. "So what exactly are you guys doing?"

"There's this machine that makes her solid and non-ghostly for a supershort amount of time. That's the thing I was trying to pull up out of the floor before you barged in."

"Well, what are you waiting for?" Poppy asked, leaning over to watch him work on the board. After a few minutes Dahlia felt her molecules go back to normal. She drifted up toward the ceiling, doing a happy little air-flip to celebrate.

Down below her, Poppy let out a startled yelp. "Hey! Where'd she go? She was here, like, a second ago!"

"Shush already," Oliver said with an exasperated groan. "If you're going to stay, you might as well make yourself useful. Grab the other side of this board." He tossed down the crowbar and the two of them hoisted up the long plank.

"Whoa, look at that! It's a . . . wait, what is it? It's *old*!"

Oliver reached into the empty space under the floor and pulled out the device.

"Seesaw," Poppy said, running her finger along the words on the side. "Is this the de-ghosting machine, huh? Oliver? Is this it?"

"Poppy, if you don't calm down I'm not going to tell you a single thing."

Dahlia looked at them, and then at the Seesaw. She slid down a moonbeam and landed right in between them—still

invisible to their eyes, she knew. She hated giving up her
ghostly form, even for such a brief time. But these living kids
were the only hope she had. Oliver was right: that Wiley guy
wasn't going to be talked into giving up the prize he had waited
for so long. Something new had just occurred to her, though.
If she found her Anchor, wouldn't the Ghouncil *have* to get
involved? They would call for Mrs. Tibbs, would see what had
happened to her and send some kind of reinforcements to the
rescue. Hadn't Mrs. Tibbs said the Ghouncil was kind of like
the police? Well, there you go. And getting free of the Boundary would also mean that *she* could follow Wiley home and try
to figure out some way to help.

It wasn't the most foolproof plan, but it was a start. The
biggest thing was it all had to happen *soon*. In spite of Oliver's
assurances, she didn't think he'd be able to keep Rank Wiley
on the premises for long.

Dahlia reached out her hand and stuck it into the center of
the Seesaw. It was going to be a long night, and she had a complicated story to tell.

Chapter 18

Oliver woke the next morning feeling like a truck had run over his head. Then he realized he was lying on the narrow strip of Matchbox floor, and Poppy was flopped across his bed, her foot resting smack on the bridge of his nose. He sat up, blinking. For a second he couldn't remember why he was so tired, but as soon as he did, he jumped to his feet. The ghost, Dahlia! The other one, Mrs. Tibbs, sucked away into captivity! And Rank Wiley and his evil device! He had to get to work.

Jabbing Poppy in the ribs—she was lucky he didn't shove her on the floor, after she'd stolen his bed like that—he shook out his shirt and smoothed down his jeans so it didn't look quite so much like he'd slept in his clothes. Not that Mom was likely to notice these days, with her one-track Party Zombie mind.

"Hunnnh?" Poppy said groggily, sitting up. "Where am I? Why's my room turned into a teeny-tiny box?"

"Get up," said Oliver. "You're in *my* room. And we need to

save the ghosts, remember? I have to go make sure Wiley doesn't leave. You start looking for clues."

"Good morning to you too!" Poppy yawned and slid out of bed. "So, that was quite a story last night, huh? Did we ever figure out what type of clues we're looking for?"

Oliver was already at the door but stopped to look back at her. "No idea. She said they've already searched the house. I don't know what we could find that they didn't, except . . . when she was talking I kept thinking about the house itself. Silverton Manor. Remember that curse we keep hearing so much about?"

Poppy perked up. "Yeah?"

"Dahlia had no idea where that rumor started or why. It seems like *something* must have kicked it off. Maybe you can find out about that?"

Leaving Poppy to digest her new mission, Oliver dashed down the attic steps and began the long trek toward the first-floor guest bedroom. When he was halfway down the second-floor hallway, something shot out of a far corner and zipped right under his foot. He swerved to avoid it, saving himself from stepping on it just in time. Bending down he saw an old-fashioned roller skate with long straps dangling off the sides and a yellow smiley face beanbag filling the base of it.

"JJ!" he called, looking around for his offending siblings. They were nowhere to be seen, but gleeful cackles from around the corner confirmed his suspicions. He pushed the skate back toward the noise and continued down the hall.

He came upon Wiley a minute later, his long legs sprawled out across the hallway. What on earth? Rank Wiley leaped up in a flash, looking first alarmed, then annoyed when he saw it was Oliver. He was busily stuffing a tiny camera into a messenger bag on his shoulder.

"Mr. Wiley," Oliver said, swallowing all the extremely unpleasant things he wanted to say. It was hard enough to make his voice sound friendly, without having to say nice stuff too! He took a deep breath and tried again. "Are you packing up all your hidden ghost cameras?"

"I am rather flush with success at the moment, if you don't mind," Wiley said smugly, turning around and starting down the hall toward the stairs. "Seems like high time to move along, set my sights, focus on the next goal—that is, to begin dissecting the evidence." Up ahead of them, Oliver thought he heard a telltale giggle. He brightened. Maybe he wouldn't *need* to say anything nasty to get a nice little bit of revenge. Maybe if he kept the ghosterminator distracted . . .

Wiley walked on a few steps and then apparently decided that talking to an annoying boy was better than no one at all. He beckoned and Oliver scooted closer, eyes darting from side to side. The edge of a red hair ribbon stuck out from around a corner right ahead of them. "I am confident," Wiley intoned as they walked, "that the evidence I've collected this week— culminating in the remarkable capture of a live specimen!— will catapult me to international fame and fortune. I will be immortalized forever. I'm Rank T. Wiley, my boy, and the *T* stands for *Timeless*. Timeless! And if I should be able to discover what comprises the essence of those creatures, well!"

The man's eyes took on a faraway look. Oliver kept his own eyes on the ground. Even so, he almost missed the gentle *whir* as the smiling roller skate scooted out from behind a dark corner, sliding neatly under Wiley's foot. Busy contemplating his future importance and worldwide acclaim, Wiley brought his foot down with purpose. *Slam* went the foot and *zip* went the skate and *whoosh!* went the ghosterminator.

It was the most impressive tumble Oliver had seen yet. Wiley slid a full six feet down the hallway, teetered on the edge of the rounded staircase, then gave in to gravity and toppled onto his backside. *Boom, boom, boom!* It seemed impossible, but Wiley managed to bounce on his behind all the way down the sixteen steps leading to the living room. Obviously unhurt but bright red with embarrassment, Wiley leaped to his feet at the foot of the staircase. He shook his fist at Oliver.

"You scheming scoundrel! You rotten shrunken head!" he bellowed.

Oliver immediately swallowed his laughter and dashed down the stairs. He still had to deliver his message.

"Wait, Mr. Wiley," he said, reaching the landing slightly out of breath. "I'm so sorry about your fall. I had nothing to do with it, I promise! But about the ghost stuff . . . I, er, wonder if there might not be more things you could find before you go. Outside, maybe?"

Wiley took two steps but seemed off-balance. He lifted his

shoe and there, stuck to the bottom, was the grinning yellow beanbag. Wiley yanked it off angrily. "I repeat: I've gotten what I came for and I will not stay in this abominable house for another minute!" He hurled the beanbag across the room—

Where it connected with the center of Mom's face. Yellow smiley face wiggling on the tip of her nose, Mom was momentarily stunned. A chorus of delighted laughter came from the upper landing, where JJ's prank had garnered the best results ever, and Oliver shuddered at how this would shape their future life of crime. But in an instant Mom swiped the beanie smile off her nose. She marched over to Wiley, hands on her hips.

"You are going precisely *where*, Mr. Wiley?" she snapped. "Have you inspected the heating system, as agreed upon yesterday? What were the results of this inspection and what is next on your to-do list?"

Wiley cowered. "Of course, Mrs. Day. The boiler and the heating vents are all in perfect running order—I inspected them thoroughly myself and they could not be in better condition. Ship as ship-shape, in fact. As to the other work . . ." He wrung his hands regretfully. "I truly wish I could stay longer. But the fact is that I've received an urgent call from a client who—"

"Mr. Wiley, *I* am your client right now and I am telling you that your work is not yet complete. Come right this way—I have two tasks which must be taken care of immediately in preparation for tomorrow's party."

Oliver took one step backward, then another, moving very

quietly and stealthily. A sigh of relief escaped him. Wiley wasn't going anywhere for a while; Mom would see to that. Satisfied, he started to run toward his room.

But just as quickly he realized that his running feet weren't moving anywhere: a hand had ahold of the back of his collar. "Young man," Mom said. Could her arm really stretch that far? Oliver turned around. It was Party Zombie Mom all right, with one hand on his shirt and the other gripping Wiley's sleeve, making sure her two latest victims couldn't get away.

"Decorations," Mom said to Oliver. "I've ordered a bunch of supplies and piled them all up in the living room. Poppy's in there getting started, so that's a task for the both of you: by the end of the day tomorrow I want this house to look thoroughly haunted."

Oliver gulped. "Haunted?" He glanced at Wiley, who gave an uneasy chuckle.

"Yes, haunted!" said Mom, letting go of both shirts and waving her arms, like a conductor directing symphonies of streamers and choruses of confetti. "I want the works: spiderwebs on the ceiling, spooky lanterns in dark corners, skeletons creaking from the upper railing. A hanged mannequin, perhaps? There are some noise machines, so make sure there are evil cackles at random intervals. Beyond that . . ." She shrugged. "Be creative."

Oliver opened his mouth. "You want all that by tomorrow night?"

"Welcome to Silverton Manor," Mom said grandly. "Your very own neighborhood haunted house."

"Now look here," came a new voice in the hallway behind them. Rutabartle marched down the hall. "I hope you don't mind I came right in—the front door was open—but I couldn't help but overhear and Mrs. Day, I have to say that this haunted house business has gotten completely out of control. You assured me it would be a party—a simple affair, a neighborhood introduction. And now you seem to have this whole notion . . ."

Oliver didn't wait to hear any more. He slunk off toward the living room. Poppy was there waiting for him, looking every bit as glum as he felt but, thankfully, already channeling her hyperactivity into action. "We might as well get this out of the way," she said. She'd thrown all the dust coverings into a huge pile in the corner, and every bit of floor, couch, and coffee table space was covered in neat piles. The inside of a cereal box was propped up on the mantel, showing a rough sketch of the main gathering hall, the staircase, and the upper hallway, with appropriate decorations planned out for each.

Oliver whistled. "Wow! You've been busy."

Poppy glowered at him. "Don't you dare tell Mom. If she ever catches on that I'm good at this stuff, she'll have me doing it all the time. The important thing right now is to get it done and fast. Then we can start searching for clues." She looked shiftily from side to side. "You know . . . for the *ghosts.* And I've got some great ideas about where we can start."

*

The rest of the day passed in a blur. Oliver wondered from time to time where Dahlia was, and whether she was busy searching, or if the loss of her ghostly friend had made her too sad to do much. Somehow, Oliver didn't think so. Ghost or not, Dahlia seemed to be plenty capable, and he figured she had more than one trick up her see-through sleeves. It also occurred to Oliver that his plan to try to stay in Silverton Manor had fallen completely into the background *again*. He would get back to it soon, he told himself. Right now, the ghosts' dilemma took priority.

Still, in spite of their lightning-fast decorating pace, and even though they gobbled their lunch and barely stopped for any breaks at all, it was nearly five o'clock by the time he and Poppy hung the last streamer and sprinkled on the last coating of chalk dust.

With a groan, Oliver checked his watch. "Finally—I thought we'd never be done! We have at least another hour until dinner. Wanna start upstairs?" He wondered when Poppy had gone from pest to ally, but he couldn't deny he had been glad for her help with this decorating—and he'd be glad of her help with the searching too. Even tagalong sisters had their uses, he guessed.

"One more thing," Poppy said, with a gleam in her eye. She darted toward the living room and came back out a minute later lugging a giant mound of white cloth.

"The dust covers from the furniture?" Oliver said. "What's all that for?"

Poppy tossed him half of the pile. "You have to go around and cover all of our best decorations with this. Throw one right over the top. If it looks like we're not finished with our job yet, Mom won't give us anything else to do. We'll have all the way till tomorrow night to search. If she sees we're finished, well . . . then we're finished."

Oliver was getting more and more impressed. "I think that's the best idea I've heard all day," he said, and Poppy beamed.

Somewhere on the other side of the house, they could hear Wiley's voice rising above his mother's. "No, Mrs. Day, I most assuredly cannot. I'm grateful for your hospitality, but I cannot stay one moment longer. Yes, I *might* be able to return next week. But unfortunately, this assignment cannot wait."

Oliver looked at Poppy with wide eyes. Wiley was definitely leaving this time. What could they do? And then a thought came to him—it was risky, and he wasn't even sure it would work. But he had to give it a try. Tossing his half of the sheeting back onto Poppy's pile, he said, "You do the sheets, Poppy. I've got to take care of something."

He barely heard Poppy's shouted "HEY!" as he darted toward the main entrance and slipped out the front door into the chilly late afternoon.

Chapter 19

All day, Dahlia had been alternating between moving around the house, checking and rechecking areas they'd already searched, and using her Clearsight to keep an eye on Oliver and Poppy. But both living kids were completely absorbed with their party decorating. She could only hope that once they finished their work they could all regroup and figure out what to do next.

For her part, Dahlia favored exploring the sealed-off attic room. More and more she'd started to feel it was somehow important. She'd gone just about everywhere else, aside from the rooms filled with living people and useless living-people stuff, and it made sense that this room held some important secrets. But how could she get to them when she couldn't get inside? She'd drifted all the way around the square box of a room, running her hands along every edge of the walls surrounding it. A few times she thought she'd felt a tremor come from the room, like maybe some force was inside, keeping her out. But she couldn't figure a way in.

Outside, the late-afternoon sun was setting over the trees, and Dahlia sighed. She'd been focused on this room all day and nothing had come of it. It was time to go back to checking the rest of the house. She had to rescue Mrs. Tibbs, and to do that, she needed her Anchor.

No sooner had she thought this than the rev of an engine caught her ear. She flashed through the walls into the front courtyard, where she gasped in astonishment. With a jaunty wave and an eager step, Rank Wiley was folding his long, lean body into his tiny pickup truck.

"Yes, yes," he called, as he slammed the door shut and shifted the vehicle into gear. "I'll be back first thing on Monday, you have my word. Well, good-bye!"

Dahlia shot down onto the bed of the truck. Oh, no! He was taking Mrs. Tibbs away. What could she do? Forcing her mind into focus, she grappled with the tarp. It was tied down tight with bungee cords securing the various boxes, bags, and suitcases, and Dahlia couldn't get enough power to pry it up. Apparently, sitting on a branch was one thing and moving anything that required force was another. Or was her emotional state affecting her focus? Giving up on interacting with the objects, Dahlia shot her hand through them. There was the Spectrometer, and there was that evil black box. It burned her hand when she accidentally brushed against it, and Dahlia couldn't help wondering how Mrs. Tibbs felt inside her little prison. *How* could Dahlia get the box out of the truck? She forced all her energy on making contact with the sides of the box, concentrating as hard as she could.

Too late she realized that the truck had begun to move, and she looked quickly up. Silverton Manor's front gate hung wide open, and the truck would pass through just fine. But no opening would be wide enough to let Dahlia through. She could feel the Boundary getting closer—she punched the surface of the tarp as hard as she could—and closer—the material was fraying ever so slightly, and a tiny hole started to appear—and closer—in another second she would break through and the force of momentum would be enough for her to propel the canister out—

SLAM! The truck sped through the Boundary, and Dahlia was thrown back across the courtyard, skidding down into the ground and tangling up with a colony of expired earthworms.

The truck roared away around a far corner.

Dahlia had lost Mrs. Tibbs.

For several minutes Dahlia stayed where she was, hardly noticing that somehow she had managed to stabilize her form so she was now sitting on top of the ground. It didn't matter. Nothing mattered. What would happen to Mrs. Tibbs? Would the Ghouncil intervene, if the Liberator was away from Silverton Manor? Did they even know what had happened, and if they did, would they care? Dahlia's eyes burned and her heart ached and the world around her pulsed a dull blue-gray.

Pushing back her fears that it was over, that she had failed, that all hope was gone, she forced herself to focus on making a plan. Plan B, specifically. She'd failed to keep Mrs. Tibbs from being taken from Silverton Manor. Now she *had* to redouble her efforts to break through the Boundary, so she could leave the manor and find Wiley's house. She wasn't sure what would happen after that, but she would find a way. "There's no way my very first ghost friend is going to end up on that nasty ghosterminator's dissecting table," Dahlia said, clenching her fists and squaring her jaw.

She shot back toward Silverton Manor.

Dahlia zipped through the front door, passed through a coatrack and glanced through a silvery, shivery mirror. A buzz of voices came from the kitchen, and Dahlia slid through the walls in that direction. The whole family sat around the table, munching steadily on some sort of gooey casserole. The twins had a long ropey strand of cheese stretched between their two mouths, upon which they had strung two or three noodles. They appeared to be playing a complicated sucking game to see who could get the noodles to their own mouth first. Mr. Day was muttering to himself in a ringmaster's voice, occasionally stopping to jot something down on his paper napkin with an orange Sharpie. Mrs. Day flitted from one side of the kitchen to the other, scribbling and checking off boxes on her various to do-lists, making phone calls, putting trays into the freezer, and occasionally stopping to stuff a few noodles into her mouth.

Oliver and Poppy were shoveling down their food as fast

as they could. Their heads were bent and their faces lined up next to their bowls as if for maximum efficiency. Dahlia came up behind Oliver, focused her concentration, and jabbed him in the shoulder as hard as she could. He jumped a little, then reached over to scratch distractedly at the spot. Dahlia groaned. Despite her best efforts, she could tell it hadn't felt like more than a tickle. Why was it so hard to make Contact? She thought about dashing up to the attic and zapping herself, but how would she explain *that* to the rest of the family?

She focused on Oliver again, this time stopping to clear her mind fully and then karate-chopping down hard on his shoulder. He jumped more visibly this time, then turned and looked over his shoulder, eyes wide. He exchanged a glance with his sister. "Dahlia," she saw him mouth to Poppy, who nodded.

"Hey, Dad," said Poppy. "Can you practice your new ringmaster's speech for us? We haven't heard it all the way through yet!"

Mr. Day beamed. "Now there's an idea!" He wiped a cheesy smear off his chin, cleared his throat, and stood up. He even whipped off his hat for the occasion, holding it out like a baton. "Ladies and gentlemen," he began. "As master of ceremonies of the finest circus on this side of—"

While he spoke, Oliver leaned forward and swiped the orange Sharpie. Scooting his own napkin onto his lap he wrote, *D: We have news. Meet in attic in 5. P found—*

"Oliver," Mrs. Day interrupted, cutting off the ringmaster's speech abruptly. "How is the decorating coming along?"

"Oh, super well," Oliver began, stuffing the napkin into his pocket. "In fact, it's—"

"—taking us a bit longer than we thought," Poppy cut in smoothly. "We've got some cool ideas. It'll definitely be done in time for the party tomorrow."

Mrs. Day deflated a bit. "Oh," she said. "Oh, all right. That reminds me . . ."

Right then the phone rang. Mrs. Day grabbed the receiver, while Oliver and Poppy wolfed down the rest of their dinner. "Mr. Rutabartle! . . . Sure! . . . Well, of course. No, that's perfectly fine. How many additional guests should we expect? . . . Oh, right—ah, yes, in advance of the auction. So they can get the lay of the land? Okay, I suppose. Well, if I might add . . ."

"Come on," Oliver said, grabbing Poppy's hand, and looking around the room with a significant eyebrow wiggle, like he wanted to let Dahlia know he was leaving, wherever she might invisibly be.

"Why are you making googly eyes at the cookbooks?" Junie asked, popping the cheesy tightrope and slapping it back at Joe's face. But this was so funny that she then started laughing hysterically, and didn't notice when Oliver and Poppy slipped out of the room. Dahlia followed right behind them. She shot straight up through the floors so she was well settled in and freshly zapped by the time they cleared the top of the stairs. She settled the loose board carefully overtop of the Seesaw and wobbled into Oliver's room.

He and Poppy burst in a second later. "Dahlia," Poppy said. "Good, you're here. You'll never guess what we've found!"

But Dahlia turned right then, and could not believe what she saw: there on Oliver's bed, gleaming neon orange in the last rays of the sunset, sat Rank Wiley's Aspirator.

"Oh!" Dahlia gasped. "Where—when—how did you get that?"

"Oliver swiped it right out from under old Wiley's nose," Poppy boasted, dropping onto the bed next to it and poking the bulging sack. "That nasty man has no idea he drove away without his prize."

Could it really be? Dahlia dropped down next to the device and prodded it with a gentle finger. It was so horrible that she hated to get too close; it was also extremely weird for her now-corporeal form to be able to touch the machine that was so threatening to her as a ghost. "Mrs. Tibbs," she whispered. "Are you in there? Can you hear me?"

"Hell-o!" The voice was faint but unmistakable, and Dahlia felt her insides do a little cartwheel. Mrs. Tibbs was okay! The relief was so strong that for a second Dahlia felt the air around her roar and swell into one giant bubble of joy. Wiley hadn't moved her to the ironite box after all. "Tut-tut, my girlish gadabout, is that you out there? You've been gone for quite some time! And your voice sounds all scratchy and worn out. You aren't—"

"Oh, Mrs. Tibbs—we're going to figure a way to get you

out of there," Dahlia cut in, having a good idea what the Liberator was about to say. Sure enough:

"—doing any Dialoguing with those living children, are you? Don't forget the Ghouncil—"

"Do you suppose we could just break the machine?" Oliver asked. "Smash the canister or something and get her out that way?"

"Or look at all these buttons," said Poppy eagerly, her fingers twitching above some of the settings. "We could keep pressing until something, you know, makes it come apart? I mean, it has to come apart, right?"

"Under no circumstances should the living children tinker with this machine!" came Mrs. Tibbs's disembodied voice from inside the bag. "Dahlia, speaking to you only, please understand, I would advise you to place this receptacle somewhere safe but not attempt to mess with it. We do not know how this device works. When ironite goes bad it can . . . poison a soul."

"Poison?" Dahlia echoed, too alarmed to even smile at how Mrs. Tibbs was keeping the Ghouncil's rules by not talking directly to Oliver and Poppy.

"Yes," said Mrs. Tibbs, "and it is taking all my energy to even speak through this barrier, so I must stop now and recollect my strength. But do not attempt to get me out yourself, child. Honestly, I would suggest you forget me altogether for the time being. Find your way out of the Boundary and then contact the Ghouncil to intervene. They do like being called in as experts, you know . . ." Her voice trailed away, and Dahlia suddenly noticed that she herself was almost fully ghost-solid again—which she knew meant that to the living kids, she would be disappearing.

"Hey, don't go," Poppy said to her. "We've got something else to show you. I found some old papers in my room that are pretty cool."

"Can you go back through the Seesaw?" Oliver asked. "So we can look through this stuff together?"

Dahlia was more excited than she'd been all day. Mrs. Tibbs was safe—even if there was no way to get her out yet, at least Wiley couldn't hurt her—and now there were new clues! Things were looking up. Fully restored to her own ghostliness, Dahlia shot through the walls, plunged her hand into the floorboard, and zapped herself again.

But something was different this time. The jolt was quicker, but it felt strange somehow, like falling and scratching a knee that already had a scab on it. She felt herself turn corporeal, but she also felt suddenly exhausted, her newly physical body much heavier than usual.

"I bet I'm using it too often," she murmured. "It can't be good for me." Yet she had no desire to slow her usage. This was a tool, a gift she'd been given. She had to find any available information, and she didn't have long to do it. Whatever the price, she was willing to pay it. Just as long as she could solve the mystery of her death and discover a way to break through the Boundary.

Chapter 20

Oliver leaned back on the bed, hands behind his head. Poppy was totally boasting about her discovery, but he had to admit it was a sweet find. "There was this bookshelf in my room and when I moved in I just piled my princess collection overtop of the junk that was already there. You know, who has time to do all the sorting and cleaning and junking stuff out, right?" She rolled her eyes. "Anyway, I did remember there was a ton of paper there, so after I finished draping all those sheets today—" Here she shot Oliver a dark look and he grinned back. "I went to see what I could find. And . . . ta-da!"

She thrust out a leather binder stuffed with crinkly, yellowing pages. Putting the folder in Dahlia's hands, Poppy sat back on the bed, beaming.

"This is remarkable!" Dahlia whispered, sitting down next to Poppy on the bed. "I didn't think to go through your shelves, since I thought all of that was simply your things."

Poppy nodded.

"We had a quick look through," Oliver interrupted, leaning forward. He wanted to get to the good stuff. "And it's pretty weird. You know how people in the village talk about a curse? Well, there's stuff about that in here."

Dahlia picked up a newspaper clipping and read out loud: "*Society Belle Found Dead in Youthful Prime! Laura Silverton, seventeen, was found dead today in her attic bedroom in Silverton Manor. The local Rose Cup Queen and famed beauty had been in poor health and confined to her home for the past several months with undisclosed symptoms, but officials are baffled as to the cause of death...*" Her voice trailed off. "Laura Silverton! That's one of the first names in the family Bible that Mrs. Tibbs and I saw in the library."

Oliver couldn't help noticing that Dahlia's feet were see-through. They needed to hurry up—even though she would still be able to see and hear them in her ghostly form, it wasn't the same. He reached over and picked up the papers. "There's a lot more here, especially about the curse. It looks like this girl Laura's death started the rumors, but it's much more than that. People think there's something evil about the house—there's a list that goes on and on of recorded health problems of people who've lived here: madness and weird unspecific illness and people getting sent to institutions and stuff."

"Something evil in the house?" Dahlia looked bewildered.

"Does any of this sound familiar to you? Do you remember anything about all those illnesses being in your family?"

"Nothing," she whispered. "I mean, there were all those medical books we saw in the library. Could there be a connection? Oh, this doesn't make any sense. Why can't I remember?"

"There's something else you should know," Oliver said, feeling uncomfortable. "We didn't find anything about you in this folder. Nothing at all."

"Amnesia!" Poppy yelled suddenly.

"What?" Dahlia said. She was now just a head with an upper body and arm stumps, floating gently above the bed.

Poppy rifled excitedly through the papers and pulled out a news article, which she jabbed at and yelped when her finger punched a neat hole right through it. "Oops! Well, look—see here, this list of symptoms the Silvertons have displayed over the years? Some people got amnesia as part of their illness. They said it was another part of the curse. So that must be what happened to you. That's why you can't remember, get it? You had the curse before you died, and memory loss was part of that."

"Poppy, the curse isn't real," Oliver said. "It's not like you get cursed and then get a list of symptoms. People start calling it the curse, but there has to be some logical, scientific reason. Right?" He looked at Dahlia, remembered he was speaking with a ghost, and cleared his throat quickly. "Anyway," he rushed on, "there's a lot in here, but I don't know how it all fits together. It's like there's a piece missing and I've got no idea what it is. I just think it has to be something logical, something that ties it all together."

Dahlia was studying the papers in her lap. As Oliver

watched, the pale-blue print of her dress's collar faded into air, like it was being worked on by a giant invisible eraser. Now she looked like one of those portraits in the long room down-stairs, nothing but a head and shoulders—all the more alarm-ing when the head and shoulders suddenly bounced up into the air.

"The hidden room," Dahlia said, her eyes suddenly alight. "That's the missing piece. I've been thinking a lot about that room, but look back here." She flipped to the first article. "Laura Silverton was found *in her attic bedroom*. There's no way it's this tiny room—what do you bet there's another room, hidden away behind that wall over there?"

"Wait, there's a hidden room?" Poppy said.

"Of course—there has to be," Oliver said. That explained the lack of space he'd noticed in the attic. It made perfect sense.

"If she died in that room," Dahlia continued, "that would explain why it got boarded up. Maybe that's why I can't get in. Maybe her death left some kind of energy-block in place." Dahlia turned to look right at him. "Maybe the curse comes from her."

Poppy bounded to her feet. "Let's open it up and find out. Mom loves any excuse to pull out her old tool kit." She started for the door.

"Wait!" said Oliver. "I don't think so."

"Come on, you know she would."

But Oliver shook his head. "Normally she would, but right now? She's all about this party tomorrow. If she doesn't send us straight to bed she'll think of some task for us to do. She's definitely not going to make more work for herself right now."

"But we have to get inside there!" Dahlia said, and her wide, panic-filled eyes were the only thing left visible in her now-ghostly face. "And you have to be the ones to do it—the room is blocked off to me for some reason."

"We will," said Oliver. "And we'll do it tonight. We just won't clue Mom in first."

"I'll get back to the Seesaw," said Dahlia. "I don't know how long I can keep using it, but—"

She disappeared.

Poppy turned the doorknob and stepped into the hallway. "I'll go get the toolbox. We'll find a way in, no problem."

Alone in the Matchbox, Oliver looked around. "I wish I knew where you are when you're invisible," he said. "It gives me the creeps not knowing what you're up to." He swiveled his head from side to side. He felt a prickling in his right shoulder and swatted at it. A second later there was a light scratching sound from the window. The surface was slightly steamed up. Oliver took a step closer to the window and grinned as two tiny stars appeared in the condensation of the windowpane, then below it a wide, half-moon smile.

·Getting into the closed-up attic room turned out to be easier than Oliver had expected, though their plan to tackle it that night quickly fell apart. First Mom stopped by Oliver's room lecturing about the big day tomorrow, then Dad with JJ in tow demanding a slumber party. By the time they had all left, JJ bribed with future promises, Oliver couldn't keep his eyes open. Poppy crept into his room just after midnight, looking more than halfway asleep herself. They agreed to start first thing in the morning.

Particularly since they were opening the room of a dead girl, someone who might have somehow brought down a curse, daylight seemed like a good idea.

"Poppy," Oliver said through a yawn, "you were right after all—you know, about the spooky-weird, not just the cool-weird."

"Duh, I'm always right. You should know that by now. But you were right too."

"Huh?"

Poppy grinned. "We *have* to find a way to stay in this house. As soon as all this ghost stuff is over. Night!" She leapfrogged over the banister and disappeared down the hallway.

They set to work immediately after breakfast the next morning. Although Dahlia wasn't able to ghost through the wall of the hidden room, she used something she called Clearsight to look through the wallpaper, and found a door buried under a couple layers of the brightly patterned paper.

"Right here," she said, marking the spot on the door with her hands after going through the zapper. This time, she came back moving extra slowly, like she had a heavy backpack on her shoulders, and Oliver hoped it wasn't hurting her to keep using that machine.

Poppy dove for the box cutter, but Oliver got to it first. "Mom would kill me if I let you use this without her permission," he said, elbowing his sister out of the way. It didn't take much effort to cut a door shape out of the checkered wallpaper. Dahlia showed them where to cut, though when she was visible she didn't have her ghost sight, so some of the edging was off. Still, in less than fifteen minutes the door was visible. Oliver got a wrench and stuck it through the empty hole where the doorknob had been removed.

He turned the wrench and pulled the door toward him. It swung open wide.

Chapter 21

The hidden room was beautiful. Dahlia gazed in through the slowly opening doorway and something shivered inside her, something like a bud lifting its tiny head to the light, opening one petal and then another. So this was the mysterious cursed room! Why did it feel so . . . comforting? She looked around for signs of ghostly energy, but couldn't see or hear anything out of the ordinary. Of course, she was still fully corporeal, so maybe she wouldn't see anything until she resumed her true form.

She took in the high poster bed—dull and worn with age, pink satin trim just visible under the thick layer of dust, but gleaming shimmery silver in the early morning light from the far window. A tall, ornate chest of drawers filled one wall, and a plush carpet was spread across the floor.

Almost without registering what she was doing, Dahlia's

feet began to move through the open door and across the floor, her eyes running over every detail.

"Hey," Oliver said. "Didn't you say you . . . couldn't come in this room?"

Dahlia felt a sudden lurch in her insides. "I did say that—I couldn't—"

And yet, here she was. The room that had been blocked to her as a ghost had let in her non-ghostly form. Oliver seemed to understand and returned to exploring, and Poppy was fiddling with a music box. Dahlia turned her attention toward the bed. Right next to it, something hung on the wall. She walked over to it and blew off a cloud of dust. It was a wide, flat calendar of yellowed cardstock. At the top, she read, *The Star Lover's Guide to 1954.*

Dahlia swallowed. What was it about this place? Why did it seem almost familiar?

"Wow!" Poppy's gasp was so loud that Oliver's hand shot out to shush her. Their parents might be two floors and multiple rooms away, but sound had a way of carrying the best when you least wanted it to.

Strange feelings rushed through Dahlia as she watched Poppy brush dust off the coverlet and lift up the edge to peer at the sheets. Oliver walked over to the dresser and pulled open the top drawer. He wrinkled his nose. "Clothes," he said. "Old ones. Lots of lace and stuff."

Dahlia was growing more and more confused at the strange feelings churning inside her. "Wait," she whispered, but the other two didn't hear her. Poppy had her hand on a wooden chest that sat under the window. Suddenly Dahlia couldn't take it anymore. She felt a rush of emotion welling up inside her, so hot and fast and strong she could hardly contain it. She ran across the room and yanked Poppy away from the chest. "Stop!" she said. "Just leave everything alone!"

Poppy turned around and raised an eyebrow.

Dahlia found that she was trembling. What was going on with her? There was some connection here, something about this place she could almost remember but not quite. Some draw pulling her just as strongly as the fear was trying to push her away.

"Never mind," she muttered, moving toward the bed. "Just jittery, I guess." Her legs looked sharply outlined again, so she knew the others saw her bobbing around on a short floating skirt. She didn't have much longer before her next zap.

"It looks like the room was frozen in time," Oliver said. "Somebody locked it up years and years ago, after Laura Silverton's death, I guess. And no one's set foot in it since."

"No kidding," Poppy said, waving her dust-blackened hands and turning back to continue investigating.

Dahlia ran her hand along the edge of the coverlet, gently swirling the dust up into the air. The bed was neatly made, with a folded pile of clothing on the end. Almost as though it was still waiting for the room's inhabitant to wake up and get dressed. Dahlia sat down on the bed, and her eyes fell on the nightstand.

Reaching over, she picked up a tiny silver frame. She blew the dust off the frame and saw a tiny black-and-white photograph containing three fuzzy, washed-out faces: a wide bearded man, a stern but smiling woman, and a small apple-cheeked girl.

Dahlia's hands turned invisible. The picture frame dropped through them, clattering to the floor. Her breath catching in her throat, Dahlia jumped up and shot back toward the main storage area. She had to get back to the Seesaw, had to zap herself again as quickly as she could, and then start searching that room from top to bottom. Because, because—

The small face in the frame was her own.

This had been *her* room.

How could she not have known it? And yet, of course, she now realized that somewhere deep down, she *had* known. Right from the start, bits of knowledge had been there, little tendrils of remembrance. She thought of the date on the calendar—far later than Laura Silverton had lived. She thought of her discomfort at the others fingering the things in the room—*her things.*

"What's the matter?" Oliver asked behind her as she finally slowed to a stop, hovering over the loose board.

Dahlia bent over to pick up the Seesaw but her hands passed right through it. The jolt caught her off guard—was she growing so used to Manifesting that she was forgetting she was a ghost?—but once her form stabilized, she steadied herself and picked up the device. Might as well bring it back to the room, as she would certainly need to use it again soon.

"That closed-up room was yours, wasn't it?" Oliver asked. "It wasn't that Laura girl's after all. You were a lot younger in that photo, but it's definitely you."

Dahlia walked back toward the room on leaden feet. "I don't know anything about Laura, but I do remember this being my room. It just . . . the memories came back to me all at once. I'm sure we'll find some clues in here." She paused on the threshold. "Or, I hope we will. I don't think I was in here when I was young. It was much later. I do remember my early child-hood years, you know. My memories don't stop until a year or two before I died, until . . ." The memory came to her like a slap across the face. "Until my father left. That's when everything changed—I can almost remember. My mother pulled back into herself. I hardly saw her. She let most of the household staff go. She became kind of like a ghost herself."

Oliver looked down at the ground. If he was uncomfort-able hearing all this personal stuff, he didn't show it. He just looked sad.

Dahlia shook her head. "Come on, let's get searching. Your party is going to start soon, isn't it?"

She stepped through the door, with the Seesaw clutched tightly against her chest. As she crossed the threshold, though, something felt different. There wasn't a wall keeping her out, like when she was a ghost, but something was pushing against her, holding her back like a web, like a soap bubble and with just a bit more pressure . . . the push became an energy, which pulled suddenly taut. Dahlia leaned in harder, and finally it burst in a gush that knocked her backward.

There was a loud grinding noise, as if the walls themselves might be coming apart. The floor lifted and dropped, shook itself like a dog, then was still. Dahlia barely kept her balance, panting a little.

She knew what had just happened: she'd broken through the force that had kept her out of the room while she was in her ghost form. When she was back to normal, she knew she would be able to use her Clearsight and see right through this room, just like any other part of the house. But why? And how?

Had she just broken the curse?

Arms shaking, Dahlia set the Seesaw on the ground inside the door.

"What *was* that?" Poppy asked. "Are you okay? You went all white and the room kind of went boom and jiggled. Do you think anyone downstairs heard that?"

"I sure hope not," said Oliver.

"Is everything all right up there?" Mrs. Day's voice drifted up the stairs, sounding thankfully far-off.

The kids exchanged looks. "Fine!" called Oliver quickly. "Just, uh, dropped something heavy. No problems here!"

A rumbling man's voice chimed in. "Perhaps we should make sure all is well."

"Rutabartle?" Poppy whispered. "What's that nosybones doing here?"

"Checking up on the party, probably," said Oliver.

Poppy giggled. "Do you think he'll like our decorations?"

Dahlia wanted to join in the lighthearted conversation. She also wanted to think about this question of the curse and the dispelled energy and what that would mean for the Day family. Instead, all she could think of was that she was standing in this room, in *her very own room*, walking on the floors that she had walked on before she died. Maybe the actual *room* where she had died.

It was like a blanket had been lifted off the air surrounding her and it now hummed and whispered to her in soft, familiar tones. She dove back into her search with a renewed energy.

"Papers," Oliver told Poppy, also busy searching once again. "Like a journal, or photographs, anything that could be a keepsake. Holler if you find anything." He was over by the window, opening up the wooden chest that rested below the sill.

"I'll take the dresser," Dahlia said, feeling she didn't want anyone else pawing through her underclothes.

Poppy lifted the bedskirts and started burrowing underneath. "Musty stockings," came her muffled voice. "Some kind of lace napkin, uh, handkerchief? A wooden ball . . ."

"We don't need a running commentary, Poppy. Just tell us about stuff that looks important." Oliver closed the chest and moved over to pull a wicker basket out from under an antique rocking chair.

Dahlia sifted through drawer after drawer, but with the exception of some very fine undergarments, didn't find anything of interest. One starched pinafore in a blue poinsettia pattern made a lump rise in her throat. She almost remembered a package coming in the mail, her father's familiar handwriting scrawled over the label . . . she remembered the hurt that stormed across her mother's face, her own eager thrill as she pulled the dress out of the package.

She held it up now: it might have fit a small eight-year-old, and some bits of leftover memory told Dahlia that she had passed her twelfth birthday when the dress had arrived. The mix of being remembered and yet so misremembered had been a crushing blow. Yet, looking closer, Dahlia could see that careful snips and stitches had changed the fabric. It was no longer the pinafore of her memory. This had been painstakingly worked over by—she looked closer—by *childish* fingers. She herself must have transformed the too-small dress into a frilly top that would fit her just right.

But she suddenly knew something with absolute certainty: she had never actually worn the top. It was like the rest of her past life—not quite right to begin with, nearly fixed, but ultimately left forgotten in some dark corner. And suddenly it was all too much. Dahlia gripped the fabric and ripped it clean down the middle.

"Hey," said Poppy, darting over to her side. A long dust

bunny dangled off the end of her ponytail. "What are you doing? What is that?"

"Nothing," Dahlia muttered, ripping it again. "Just some old"—*rip*—"long-forgotten"—*rip*—"completely useless piece of—"

"Wait," Oliver said gently, pulling the fabric from her hands. But it was too late. The pieces were tiny and as they drifted down to the wood floor, past her now-ghostly legs, she saw the sharp image of the expired top pulling away. Instinctively she reached up her hands to catch it, looking down at her outfit and wondering whether it wasn't too late to try it on, to reclaim some piece of her former self. But her hand—still corporeal from the last Seesaw jolt—passed right through. The lump in Dahlia's throat grew as the blue-patterned top slipped through the attic ceiling and was gone forever.

She took a moment to compose herself. "Never mind that," she said at last, trying for firmness but unable to keep a wobble out of her voice. "It's just some old stupid part of my past."

Oliver looked unconvinced, but Poppy jabbed him aside. She grabbed Dahlia's hand, tugging it gently in her own. "I had this splinter one time," she said. "Oliver said it was stupid baby stuff but it wasn't, it was big and jagged and it hurt like crazy. I didn't want anyone to touch it and, okay, I went nuts when Dad got out his tweezers. But you know . . ." She scuffed at the floor with her shoe. "It had to get worse before it could get better. It hurt to get it out . . . but then, in the end, it was better."

Dahlia blinked. And then she smiled slowly. "Okay," she said. "Okay."

Beside her, Oliver was looking at Poppy with surprise. Then he turned to Dahlia. "You've remembered your past then?"

"Not everything. I've got some bits and pieces, but I need to remember how I died. I suppose that's the splinter I need to dig out. And I think the only way I can remember everything is to find my Anchor."

"What about that big bump before, when we came in here the second time?" Poppy asked. "What was that about?"

"I don't know. It felt . . ." Dahlia stretched her mind back. "Like some kind of energy force. Like something not all the way there. Not completely whole."

"Could the energy have just vanished? Gone out into the air?" Oliver asked.

"I don't think ghostly energy can just, um, dissipate. It's not like an actual ghost that would cross over—these kinds of energies have to go somewhere else. Matter won't just disappear, even ghost matter."

"So do you think it's got anything to do with that Laura person, like we thought?" Poppy asked. "Or with the curse?"

"Again with the curse," Oliver said with a groan.

Dahlia smiled wanly. "It can't be a ghost—I'd have seen her if she hadn't crossed over. All I know is that this force or curse or whatever it is has been trapped in here for a very long time. And now it's out."

"It's out?" Poppy said. "Oh, man. We've set the curse loose in the house, haven't we? And just in time for the party too!"

And that was when they noticed that the clomping and banging they had been hearing for the last few minutes was not ghostly at all, but consisted of footsteps climbing the attic stairs. This was followed by the voice of Jock Rutabartle: "What is all this talk I'm hearing about ghosts and haunting and a curse being loose in the house?"

Chapter 22

To Oliver, Rutabartle sounded more annoyed than angry, like they should know better than to make haunting jokes in a normal house that was soon to be sold to and inhabited by normal people. "Be cool," Oliver whispered to the others. "He can't possibly guess what we were really talking about—he'll think we were just goofing off."

"Oliver? Poppy?" Mom was in front, and she came up the stairs at a brisk pace, with Rutabartle immediately behind her. "Good, you're both here. I've set out a cold lunch downstairs and as soon as you've eaten I want you to change for the party. Guests may begin arriving as soon as three o'clock, and that's not much time at all. More likely not until five, but one can never be too careful. Isn't that so, Mr. Rutabartle?"

Rutabartle stood frozen in place. His eyes bulged and his face looked like it was being colored in with an invisible red crayon. Wait, invisible? *Oh!* Oliver gasped and turned quickly around, in the direction both Mom and Mr. Rutabartle were now staring with open mouths. Next to Poppy hung the old-fashioned torso, right arm, and smiling face of Dahlia Silverton.

"Is ... that—is that ... tell me, are any of you seeing that ... ," Rutabartle stammered.

"Good grief," said Mom, bringing her hands together with a sharp clap. "Have you two found yourself a ghost? Do you have a name, dear? You aren't a projection, are you? Oliver? Are you fooling around with us?"

"I'm Dahlia Silverton, ma'am," said Dahlia, sounding rather wispy as her remaining arm disappeared and the nothingness started to chew up toward her neck.

Mom started slowly circling around Dahlia. "And you seem to be ... disappearing? Is that supposed to happen? Are you all right?"

"Oh, well—yes. It's because of the—"

"Just the way things are! With ghosts!" Oliver cut in quickly. He didn't like the way Rutabartle's face had gone from red to white and was now inching toward green. Bringing up the Seesaw right now was probably not the best idea.

"She's nice," said Poppy. "We're trying to help her remember how she died. We opened up the secret room, see?"

Mom seemed to notice the sliced-through wallpaper for the first time. She ran her finger along the dusty wall and frowned. "You shouldn't have disturbed things without asking me." She tilted her head toward Rutabartle, whose mouth was now opening and closing in an obvious attempt to bring his brain up to speed with what was going on.

With a barely noticeable *snick*, Dahlia's face winked out. As if that were the last straw in a whole hayloft of offenses, Rutabartle exploded. "WHAT IN THE NAME OF NORMALCY IS GOING ON IN THIS HOUSE?" he roared. "Have you given no thought AT ALL to the instructions so clearly stated in my Normalcy Questionnaire?"

Mom took a step back, but Rutabartle was just getting started. "It's bad enough that pranks are being pulled around every corner, and that you display the very worst possible taste in party decorations. Now your reprehensible family has the gall to launch some sort of ghostly projection? Do you really think I'm going to fall for this type of trick, after all the time I've spent planning for this sale, after everything I've put into it? Can you even begin to imagine—"

"Mr. Rutabartle!" Mom said frostily. Her voice wasn't even raised, but it silenced Rutabartle for a second.

Only for a second, though. He shook his head, and a steely look came into his eye. "Very well. You leave me with no alternative." He whipped out his planner and began to flip through the pages. With his other hand he pulled out his phone and pressed a button. "Hello, Greta? Yes, it's me. No, this is urgent. Drop everything else you're doing. Yes? No, that too. It's about the auction."

Oliver took a step forward. "Please, wait," he said.

"Yes," Rutabartle went on, taking a step farther into the

hidden room and raising his voice, like it was part of their collective punishment to hear every word of what was going to
happen. "No, I realize it was supposed to be held in April. But
there have been some unforeseen developments, and we need
to send out an emergency update. Hmmm? Oh no, I don't think
so. I believe we can turn this to our advantage—catch people
off guard, so to speak. Spike up the enthusiasm, you know. I
want you to start making calls immediately. We'll hold the auction at the house sitters' Halloween party. We'll hold the auction
tonight."

The words hung in the still attic air, echoing in the confined
space and bouncing up to the narrow ceiling space and coming
back down to land on Oliver's head like a ton of bricks. All his
plans, all his hopes, all his dreams—they were all going to come
to nothing. So much for having time to plan, to scheme, to save
up more money. He'd counted up the coins in his jar and they
came to a grand total of $89.21. Not even a hundred times that
much would be enough to buy the house. And not only were
they not going to get to stay in the house for good—now they
weren't even going to get their six months!

He wondered where Dahlia was and what she was thinking
right now. Rutabartle had finished his call and stood, grinning
smugly, as though satisfied to have gotten one up on his ghost-
loving house sitters.

Then Mom's voice broke through the strained silence. "Mr.
Rutabartle, we signed a six-month contract. You cannot simply change deadlines around to suit yourself!"

Rutabartle jutted out his chin and stroked his mustache. "I think you'll see if you look at the contract carefully, Mrs. Day," he oozed, "that there is a small-print clause that stipulates a stay of six months *or until such a time as the property ownership should pass to anyone other than the current principal.* You will be given thirty days after the sale to collect your belongings and find other employment. And then"—he drew himself up with a chill smile—"you can hit the road."

"We didn't bring Dahlia into your stupid house," Poppy steamed, marching up and standing so close to Rutabartle that she had to tilt her head all the way back to glare at him. "And she's not a projection, either. She was here before we came, and all we're doing is helping her."

Oliver wasn't sure if it was better or worse for their case that Rutabartle didn't believe Dahlia was real. Not that it would make much difference either way, it seemed. He couldn't think of a single thing to say to make things better.

Rutabartle reached into his front shirt pocket and pulled out his mirrored sunglasses, which he slid onto his nose. He adjusted them, turning his head to either side as though taking in the view, then clapped his heels together. "I must be off," he said. "I have legally binding paperwork to draw up, an auction to organize, and a house to sell. As for *you,*" he sneered, "I suggest you all begin repacking your belongings." With that he spun around and marched down the attic stairs.

"Oh," Mom said. Her knees seemed to give way, like a

balloon leaking air, and she dropped slowly to sit on the floor. "That's a bit out of the blue. Who would have thought it? I suppose we had better tell your father."

"Mom," Oliver said, squatting down next to her. Silverton Manor was supposed to be *their* house. This couldn't be the end of it. "We haven't lost yet! He's going to hold an auction, but do you really think anyone's even going to bid? Think about it! What about the curse?"

"Yeah!" said Poppy. "We even found papers and news clippings and stuff. The curse is real! Plus, the house is haunted. Who wants to live in a haunted house?"

"Haunted?" chirped a voice. "Did somebody say 'haunted house'?" Oliver hadn't even heard the telltale pitter-patter of feet, but now JJ burst unexpectedly above the attic threshold in a wild explosion of freckled enthusiasm.

"A new bedroom! Look, there's a new bedroom!" they chorused. "We want to go inside!" They had somehow learned to time their jumping so that when one was up the other was down, and vice versa, and they could go on like this for full twenty-minute intervals. Mom leaped up and put a hand on each of their heads to keep them grounded. Doing this seemed to jerk her back into her businesslike self.

"Well, there's nothing we can do about all of this for the moment," she said briskly. "All we can do is finish our job with dignity. I, for one, intend to see this party through and leave with my head held high. Wouldn't you agree, children?"

Oliver wasn't sure he agreed at all, but he knew what Mom wanted from him so he gave a reluctant nod. He noticed Poppy didn't even give that, but Mom didn't press the issue.

"Now," she said, grabbing JJ firmly by the hands. "Shall we head downstairs and make sure everything is ready for our guests? I'll need you all to come and change into your party clothes too."

"Moooom," Poppy whined.

"New bedroom!" said Junie. "I want to stay in the new bedroom!" She was jumping a little again, and Mom's arm flopped up and down with her.

"Sleepover!" Joe trilled like the world's most annoying freckled bird.

Mom looked down at her watch, and up at Oliver's and Poppy's gloomy faces. "You won't want to hang around the party for long, will you?" she asked.

Poppy snorted.

"SLEEPOVER!" chorused JJ.

Mom peered around the room. "It's awfully dusty in there. What about the portrait room? No, we'll have guests tromping all over the house, and Rutabartle will want them to look in the rooms if they're going to be putting in bids..." She sighed. She glanced over at the open door of Oliver's tiny room. "I don't suppose..."

"NEW BEDROOM!" JJ shrieked.

"Fine," said Mom wearily. "You can sleep over in here, *if* it gets a good airing out first, dust down all the surfaces—all of you—and Oliver and Poppy, you'll stay over with them?" She tried to catch Oliver's eye in a won't-you-be-a-good-older-brother look.

"Not with JJ," Poppy griped. But Oliver figured that with all the energy the twins had used up today, they would be out pretty early. And then he and Poppy could keep looking for clues. For a pesky little sister, she'd turned out to be amazingly skillful.

"Fine," said Oliver quickly. "But do we really have to make everything all nice for these stupid guests tonight? Why should we make it easy for them to buy this house out from under us?"

Mom frowned. "Oliver, you've got to understand something. Rutabartle's being very underhanded in yanking us out so quickly, but he's within his rights. We're just house sitters, honey. This isn't our house, and it never was. We have to deal with it and move on. We'll find somewhere else that's even better—you'll see."

But they wouldn't. Oliver knew that. This was *it*, the house of his dreams, the only place he wanted to move into and live for the rest of his life. He'd never find somewhere else like this.

And in a few hours he was going to lose it forever.

Chapter 23

Dahlia felt adrift. Mrs. Tibbs was gone. Her Anchor was nowhere to be found. And now her new friends, Oliver and Poppy, were being booted out of Silverton Manor. In a few weeks she'd be completely alone again, like before. Only now that she'd had friends, even for this short time, she knew it would be worse. Much worse.

Dahlia dropped down into the house, through floors and ceilings, passing through a potted plant that, even with its scratchy chlorophyll insides, didn't give her a boost; passing through a cobwebby decoration, through the far corner of the kitchen and into the mudroom. What was the point? What could she hope to do? Everything she'd tried to accomplish seemed to go wrong—in fact, she had the distinct feeling she was continually making things worse rather than better.

And then a scuffling noise drew her attention. Looking up, she caught the mudroom door closing behind someone.

Someone who trailed a sort of black cloud in their wake. Dahlia looked more closely through the door.

Hat pulled down low over a bushy head, long lean body hunched over as though trying to be as unnoticeable as possible, Rank Wiley passed through toward the back hallway.

Rank Wiley? What was *he* doing here?

Oh. Of course. He must have realized his Aspirator was gone. He'd come back for Mrs. Tibbs.

The thought galvanized Dahlia into action. She suddenly realized that not only was all not lost, there was still more she could end up losing if she wasn't careful.

"Fine," she said, grinding her teeth up into a determined sort of smile. "It's not the end of the war, just the start of a new battle."

With that she propelled herself into a mini ghostwhirl and shot back up toward the attic. First she would give herself a good zap, then she'd go tell Oliver and Poppy that Wiley was back. Maybe she could even find a way to stop him herself. After all, he couldn't Aspirate her if she was in living form, could he?

Could he? She didn't think so, and at any rate, it was the only idea she had.

She reached the Seesaw in a few seconds and eagerly plunged her hand through the surface, waiting for the *zap* that would tell her she'd become visible to living eyes.

But nothing happened.

She put her hand through again. Nothing. She tried the

other hand. Nothing. Desperately, she flipped over and waggled her head around inside of it. But not even a crackle of energy lit the clunky old machine, which sat there as dead as any non-expired doornail.

Dahlia's thoughts were in a panic. What had happened? The last time she'd stuck her hand through there had been no problems . . . a little tiredness, heaviness, but no signs of it not working!

She thought back to the energy burst she'd felt when she entered the room with the Seesaw. Was there some connection with the breaking of that barrier and the breaking of the Seesaw? If so, the timing could not be worse.

Oliver and Poppy were nowhere to be seen, either. Oliver's jeans and T-shirt were scattered halfway in and out of his room. She guessed the kids were now dressed in their party best and their mom had conscripted them for last-minute prep work. Downstairs, she heard the doorbell gong ring out. The first guests must be arriving. And where was Wiley? What was he doing right now?

The Aspirator sat, fully visible in its lumpy carrying pack, on Oliver's bed.

Dahlia had never felt so powerless in her life. "Mrs. Tibbs," she whispered at the Aspirator. "Are you there? Are you all right?" But there was no reply. Mrs. Tibbs was trapped inside ironite, after all; it had probably taken all her energy just to speak out last time.

Dahlia was on her own.

Around her, the house shook a little, the walls vibrating in a low, hollow moan. She thought again of the force that had been trapped in the concealed room, which had kept her out for so long. What was it? And if it was the source of the curse, why did the energy feel more like fear than evil?

Dahlia shook her head. The more she thought, the less she seemed to understand.

Leaving Oliver's room and the Aspirator, she passed through the walls into the hidden bedroom, which still felt so familiar. She *knew* this room. And yet she still remembered so little of it. Slowing her pace and letting herself drift, she felt something. There was a distinct pulse somewhere on the edge of her senses, but she couldn't place it. She let herself sweep across the floor space: past the bookshelf, past the little writing desk, where a decades-old pen lay next to a piece of lined paper.

The pulse was clearer now. It was as though Dahlia was being pulled in a specific direction. She snapped herself into focus, and right away drifted to a stop. Where had that pull come from? It was there for a second . . . Dahlia focused. She pulled energy into herself. She gritted her teeth. *Come on!* But nothing happened.

With a great sigh, Dahlia let herself go limp again. She half-closed her eyes. And . . . yes! She started to move. She'd been trying too hard, maybe? There *was* something in this room, and if she let it . . .

She was moving toward the window. The grime-coated

pane overlooked the forest, with the roofs of Longbrook visible in the distance. There was a sudden *zing* in Dahlia's memory and she saw her own hands opening the latch, straining to lift the window, feeling a pure rush of joy as she dragged the old wooden chest over below the sill and kneeled on it to reach her head up and out. Dahlia could smell crisp autumn air filling her lungs . . . and a sharp pain that came along with it, a feel of loss or longing.

There was something else too. In that memory, she wasn't just leaning to look out the window, she was leaning *over* something. Something long and sleek, something shiny, something . . .

Dahlia felt another pulse, stronger.

It was nearby! Her Anchor.

Fluttering a little in her excitement, Dahlia tried to focus. She narrowed her eyes and sharpened her Clearsight, turning in a full circle and looking carefully through every piece of furniture in the room. Nothing called to her, and yet the pulse was still there. So close, and yet . . .

A thrum tingled through her toes, and for the first time Dahlia considered the wooden chest below her. The chest she'd been hovering above, the chest the other Dahlia of her memory had dragged over to the window ledge, had kneeled on to look out, had . . . *opened up and—*

Dahlia reached out a single ghost finger and pushed through the wooden chest-top, through a layer of crinkly-soft clothing, through a collection of papers and a few stray books . . . and there it was. Nestled in careful wrapping, lying at the very bottom of the chest was a telescope.

This! This was it.

Dahlia reached both hands through the coverings and placed them on her Anchor.

And there is love, so much love circling this shiny spyglass, this gift, this most precious of good-bye presents her daddy left with her before his last trip. He brought it wrapped in a giant box with a big red bow, and how Dahlia loved the wrapping, just as much as the telescope at first, but more important than either of those was him, *Daddy, the very best person in the whole world and the one she loved above anyone else. She'd just moved into this new attic room with the big, wide window— how long she'd wanted to, and what joy when she was finally old enough!—and he knew how much she loved that window and its view and when he handed her this present, on this night before his big trip, he said, "This is a special one, Dolly-dear, you can see far with this beauty. I want you to look out at the sky and watch the stars and know that wherever I am, I'll be look-ing at them, the same as you. For always." She'd thrilled to his words, his gift, and stayed up hours past bedtime that night, find-ing stars and constellations and whole invisible worlds she'd never thought existed.*

She'd never close her window again, she decided, not ever again. The telescope would stay pointed out through the open-ing so she could always see the stars and so she could always watch for her daddy coming home. And she did. She watched

*and watched and the days passed, summer growing from warm
to hot to scorching and then, gradually starting to frizz off into
autumn as the leaves withered and died and slowly, slowly,
something inside Dahlia started to chill too.*

*When did she first know? When Mama stopped talking about
him, stopped answering her questions, started turning away
and getting very busy whenever her usual string of questions
began? Mama never said anything, never told her that he wasn't
coming back. Not until . . .*

Dahlia jolted. Pain seared through her head. She almost,
almost didn't want to remember any more. But how could she
stop here?

*Not until the night she finally heard it for sure. He'd gone,
Mama said, he'd gone down another path and thought a clean
break would be better and easier for them all and he had called
to tell Mama but he hadn't even told his Dolly good-bye! How
could he not say good-bye? How could he leave, just up and
leave and never come back? It was too much to believe but
Dahlia believed it all too well because now she saw looking back
in her memory the determined glint in Daddy's eye, the look of
true good-bye in his last hug, the way a cold steel burned behind
his quick brisk steps as he walked away from his house, from his
life, from her. He had started a new life elsewhere.*

And he wasn't coming back.

*The moment Dahlia realized this, fully realized how com-
pletely her love had been courted and bought and then so casu-
ally thrown away, all her love hardened into hate. She ran up to*

her room and grabbed the telescope, roughly pulling it down from the windowsill. She couldn't bring herself to throw it across the room and smash it, but she shoved it into the very bottom of her trunk and slammed the lid shut. She would never touch it again. And more than that—she pulled the window shut and yanked the curtains closed. She would never again look out at that starry night sky, would never allow herself to dream stupid dreams of love and fondness and people coming back for those they cared about. She pulled the latch tightly over the window and took a deep breath and turned her back on it forever.

Dahlia came back to herself with her particles heaving and weaving in and out of focus to her blurry eyes. This was it—the Anchor, the unfinished business, the thing that had been tying her to Silverton manor. She'd found it. And yet she now felt worse than ever.

She thought of her own portrait, nestled in the dark of the attic. Was that why her mother had stored her there, safely out of sight? Had she found it simply too painful to remember the girl she had loved and lost?

Now Dahlia had all the pain, all the agony of the memory. But what she didn't have, what inexplicably had not come with the Anchor, was the last thing needed to complete her Liberation process.

She still had no idea how she had died.

Chapter 24

The rest of the afternoon and evening passed all too quickly for Oliver, who was kept busy running from one chore to another, laced in his too-tight shoes that pinched his feet and his pressed pants and his hated plaid flannel shirt. He wondered where Dahlia was, and hoped she was having a better time than the rest of them.

Once the guests started arriving, the kids were put into helper mode, offering tours to the main rooms of the house, refilling glasses and passing around trays of appetizers. Oliver wasn't sure why the appetizers couldn't stay on the side tables for people to grab themselves, but apparently this was part of the charm. Mom still held out hope that Rutabartle might change his mind—she'd obviously grown attached to the house too—but Oliver knew better. More than one group of guests he'd escorted around had muttered to themselves what an intriguing property this was, musing about prospects for future land valuation, and would this be a good investment property, all things considered? Oliver had to bite his lip to keep from offering a hundred and one reasons why this would *not* be an ideal place for them to live. But the more time passed, the more discouraged he got.

At eight o'clock, Mom trundled JJ up the stairs and whipped around the attic room with a giant duster. Oliver dragged in a pile of bedding and pulled together a bed for them. Poppy claimed the four poster, and Oliver rolled out his own mat next to the chest by the window. If all went as expected, he wouldn't be spending much time tonight sleeping, anyway.

"Now, isn't this going to be fun?" Mom said enthusiastically to JJ. "A sleepover in a secret room! I'm trusting you two to stay tucked quietly in bed, all right? Absolutely no sneaking downstairs."

"It's kind of cold up here," Poppy said, though she was swathed in old-fashioned bedding. Mom had put clean sheets on the bed, but Poppy had insisted on sleeping with the original pink satin comforter. Considering they belonged to a ghost—a dead girl—Oliver thought that was beyond creepy. But it didn't seem to bother Poppy in the slightest.

Mom squinted up at the air vent on the wall above the bed. She checked it and cleaned some dust out of the passageway, holding her hand above it. "Yes, it seems to be working. I'll go down now and turn the heat up. I can't even imagine how much it'll cost to heat this place in winter! But we won't worry about that for tonight." She frowned. "Or any night, I suppose,

since we're . . . Well! We'll get you all toasty and warm, and—
Oliver, is that window still open? Close it up right now."

Oliver pulled the window down and flipped the latch shut.
He left the curtains open, though. "Do I have to stay up here
all night, Mom? I want to see the auction."

"You will do no such thing," she said sternly. "We're on
shaky ground with Mr. Rutabartle as it is, and I don't want anything to go wrong tonight."

"Go wrong?" Oliver exploded. "How could it get any worse?
We're being kicked out of *our house!*"

"That's enough, young man," Mom said sternly. "You'll
stay here and that's final."

With those words she kissed the twins goodnight, patted
Poppy on the head, and exited the room, shutting the door
firmly behind her.

"Argh!" Oliver groaned, throwing his pillow across the
room in frustration. "How can she just stand there and do
nothing? And Dad—he didn't even say anything when he
heard the news. All he can think about is his stupid puppet
show!"

"Puppet show?" JJ perked up, peeking out of their joint
sleeping bag like a two-headed inchworm. "We want to see
the puppet show!"

Oliver sighed. "You're going to get a special showing tomorrow. I don't know why we can't go down and watch now, but
whatever."

"Well, I know why," Poppy said, and Oliver couldn't help

but smile. Poppy was right. If JJ got loose among the party guests, there was no telling what kind of trouble they would get into. Of course, that might not be *so* awful. Maybe they could scare the guests a little, lose a few potential bidders?

He sighed again. "Go to sleep, okay?" he told the twins.

They put their little noses together, gibbering away to each other, then Junie's hand shot out toward Oliver, holding something in her fist. "Here!" she chirped.

Oliver squatted down next to her. "What's this?"

She opened her hand and handed him a crumpled green piece of . . . money? It was a twenty-dollar bill.

"I grabbed it from Daddy's wallet," said Joe with a giggle. "He didn't care. He saw me and he wagged his finger."

"He was doing puppets!" Junie clapped her hands in triumph.

"We want you to have it!"

"For the house!"

"For the action!"

"Auction," said Poppy from the other side of the room. Then she frowned. "Yeah, me too. I don't want us to have to leave. I kind of love this house." She leaned over the side of her bed, where she had brought a sparkly pink overnight bag. Oliver had laughed at her for this earlier, bringing a bag to a sleepover in another room of the same house, but he wasn't laughing now. "I've been saving my pocket money for . . ."

"For years," he said. "I know, but you—" Poppy didn't spend her money for anything. Not anything. Not ice cream or toys or any of the impulse buys that had left Oliver with just coins in his coin jar. "Really?" he said.

She nodded very seriously, and put a pile of bills into his hands. She took a deep breath. "There's two hundred and eighty-five dollars there. It's all I have. Do you think it will be enough to buy the house?"

She looked so eager, so hopeful, sitting there holding the money out to him, and JJ too, with their little hands clasped around each other's shoulders, like adoring twin bugs. How could he let them down?

"I don't know," he said. He did some quick math in his head. Three hundred and ninety-four dollars and twenty-one cents was nowhere near enough to buy any kind of house, not even a crumbling old haunted mansion out in the middle of nowhere. So actually he *did* know, but he could let them dream a little longer. "Maybe I should sneak down and see if I can sit in on the auction. You never know, right?"

"Yeah!" said Junie. "You never know!"

"*I* know," said Joe, confused. Junie bopped him and they started wrestling and yanking each other's hair and howling, and Poppy dived over to get them to settle down. "Hey!" she said, motioning to Oliver to make his getaway while she tamed the wild beasts. "If you guys get quiet I'll let you up in the fancy bed!"

Oliver gave her a thumbs-up then slipped out of the door, closing it quietly behind him.

He eased down the steps, pausing as he reached the bottom of the attic stairs. A dark figure slunk around the far hallway corner. Oliver shook himself. For a second he thought he'd seen Rank Wiley! It was good that nasty ghosterminator was out of their hair, and the Aspirator safely stowed in Oliver's room. One less thing to worry about.

The guests who had wanted tours of the house had all been accommodated earlier on, and the party was now gathered in the main open area at the base of the stairs that led to the second-floor hall. Oliver found a spot on the far balcony that stretched up over the room, behind a decorative skeleton, where he could spy without being spotted. At least fifty guests were milling around, the women all decked out in floor-length gowns and the men in tuxedos. They held crystal glasses that twinkled in the light of the chandeliers. Rutabartle moved among them, speaking a word here, giving a pat on the back there, and generally mingling and working the crowd with the self-satisfied air of one for whom all is unfolding exactly as desired.

Wispy tendrils from the smoke machines hidden in the alcoves curled around the room, giving a suitably spooky-chic air to the party. Even Oliver, who knew all the behind-the-scenes tricks, was impressed.

The wall on the far side of him shook a little bit, and something let out a low moan.

The nearest guests let out a cluster of subdued giggles.

"Ohhh," said a portly lady in a spangled hot-pink dress, "that was the most realistic one yet! How *do* you manage these effects, Mrs. Day?"

Mom looked classy in her sleek black gown, but there was a blank look in her eye at that question that surprised Oliver. Well, *he* hadn't set up any shaking walls or trick noises. And it was obvious Mom didn't know anything about that either. So where had it come from? A low rumble rippled the floor.

Dahlia? Oliver thought to himself. But she'd never seemed to be *that* kind of ghost. She was more like, well, a girl who just happened to be dead. Not really into the haunting side of things, at least as far as he could see. Oliver chewed his lip.

Just then there was a loud shriek on the other side of the room, under the far rim of the balcony. What now?

He scurried down the hall to get a better view. A woman downstairs was letting out piercing yips. Something yellow oozed out of the collar of her dress.

Oliver stopped. He looked around, and—oh no! Peering over the banister partway down the staircase, was . . .

"JJ!" he hissed, dashing over to them. "What are you guys doing out of bed?"

"Did you see that?" Joe could hardly form words for giggling. "Did you hear that lady yell?"

"We used up all our goop," Junie said a little sadly.

"But for a good cause!"

"Yes! To help you make all the bad people go away."

"Then we get the house!"

"No," said Oliver.

Poppy darted up, panting and out of breath. "I've been looking everywhere for these rotten tomatoes. I feel like tossing them in the garbage can." She tucked one twin under each arm and herded them back up the hallway, muttering and scolding all the while.

Down below, the gooped-on woman seemed to have recovered. Mom was pressing a slice of chocolate raspberry tart into her hand, and a man was wiping the last of the yellow mess out of her collar. The crisis seemed to be averted.

Which was a good thing, right?

Chapter 25

Even before the Day kids started moving their blankets and sleeping bags into her old bedroom, Dahlia knew she had gotten all she could from the place. Touching the Anchor had brought back those memories of her past, but had left her no closer to freedom. What was she missing? She could still feel the walls of her Boundary on the edges of her consciousness, pulsing like an angry parent saying, *You may not leave! Not now and not ever.* It seemed more impossible that she would ever find a way out, or be able to rescue Mrs. Tibbs.

But the more she examined the problem, the more she came back to the one connection she hadn't yet fully explored. This room had been blocked since her death—or before, probably—and this was the room where her Anchor had been. Some force in this room had kept her out, until she'd brought in the Seesaw. This entity, whatever it was, had been jolted out of the room by her Manifesting machine, allowing Dahlia to enter freely in her ghostly form.

Dahlia didn't know a lot about how the ghost world worked, but she realized there was one thing she did know for sure. *Every expired object immediately began to rise.* Energy, force, entity—whatever it was, once it expired it rose and it didn't stop until it got where it was going. There was only one exception: if something—if some*one*—was Anchored in the place of their death.

Dahlia sat bolt upright. Thing 1: this had been her room, but it had belonged to someone else first—Laura Silverton. Thing 2: the force that had been in this closed-up room had not left the house; she could hear it even now shaking and rattling around in the walls. Dahlia saw no other possible explanation.

There was another ghost in Silverton Manor.

In the moment it took for the idea to sink in, Dahlia became a humming ball of energy. She hadn't seen wisp nor whirl of such a being anywhere in the house, but it was the only possible answer. She had to find this fellow spirit. She *had* to!

Her mind working at a furious rate, Dahlia studied the little attic room, watching the Day kids as they milled around and talked to each other.

For some reason the trapped presence wasn't able to—or didn't like to—materialize in the open air, so how could it now be traveling around the rest of the house? Dahlia thought of how she herself had found comfort in following living-world pathways—maybe this spirit, too, needed that kind of structure when moving through an unfamiliar place. But what kind of pathways? She scanned the room for possibilities: it was sealed as tight as a drum, from the closed window to the tiny chinks in the wall edging that had been carefully filled in with plaster. The only way out was through the slatted opening, which was now pumping out warm air.

Of course—the vents!

Another low rumble shook the walls, and Dahlia needed no further encouragement. She curled herself into a tight spiral and shot up into the heating vent. The passageway was narrow and extremely dusty. The ripples of heated air coiled over and around her like a living thing, and she swam easily through them, winding down passageways at random, her ghost ears perked for any unusual sound.

"Hello?" she called gently ahead of her. "Is anybody here?"

"Whoooooo . . ." came a sudden low howl. Dahlia stopped. She focused her Clearsight, but it didn't seem to work for finding ghosts in the way it did for living people. She closed her eyes and let herself drift. She could feel a distant thrum, a free-floating energy spike she hadn't felt before, and she let herself move toward it.

When she next opened her eyes, she was passing through an insulated partition. She felt a sharp crackle, a surge like she had felt when the attic room was closed off to her. In front of her was . . . nothing. Well, not nothing exactly. There was definitely some kind of ghostly energy, but it was as formless as a plastic bag floating underwater.

As Dahlia zeroed in, the shape started moving again. It whipped across the crowded gathering hall, upsetting a tray of puff pastry and toppling two full glasses of champagne. Several guests shrieked. Dahlia whisked after the misty gust. There was definitely someone in there; she could sense it!

"Hey," she whispered. The shapeless ghost shot into a heating vent on the floor and Dahlia followed through several walls before it slowed to a stop. The form hung motionless in front of her.

"Hello," she said again, very softly. "I'm Dahlia. Who are you?"

The form trembled. It seemed to be elongating, stretching itself into a vaguely human shape. There wasn't much room in the narrow crawl space, but Dahlia didn't want to risk pulling the being out into the open. The idea of spooking a ghost would have been funny if she'd let herself think about it. But she forced herself to stay still and wait.

The mist swirled tighter, and Dahlia could faintly see two eyes peering out of the glom. "It's okay," Dahlia said. "Nothing's going to hurt you." She reached out her hand. The presence burbled and a stringy wisp extended, slowly shaped itself into an arm, and then a hand stretched out to grasp her own hand tightly.

As Dahlia squeezed back, she focused all her energy on this new form, trying to send thoughts of quiet and peace and strength its way. She also gently pulled the ghost after her out of the cramped heating vent and into the nearby boiler room, where there was plenty of space to expand and no living folks likely to wander by.

Before her eyes, the figure took complete shape. First the eyes got less wild, settled into a soft pale-blue fringed with dark lashes; then two long, dark braids became visible. The rest of the face came slowly into focus, followed by an elaborate gown with a high lace collar and a wide fancy skirt. And then the ghost spoke.

"I am Laura Silverton," she said. "Where am I?"

So she'd been right! It *was* the girl from the article, from the family Bible, one of her ancient ancestors—who had died when she was not much older than Dahlia. And yet this answer just opened up a bunch more questions.

"Why are you still here?" Dahlia asked. "Have you been in the house this whole time?" Obviously she hadn't crossed over, and Dahlia knew as well as anyone how the Ghouncil could lose track of people who were supposed to be given help. But Laura had died well over a hundred years ago!

"I only just went to bed," Laura said slowly. She was fully formed now, and her eyes scanned the dusty room. "But where is everyone? Why does the house look so different this morning?"

Could she really not know that she had died? Had she been trapped in that formless void inside her attic room, like some kind of Sleeping Beauty who closed her eyes and woke up over a hundred years later? Only this time, there was no prince and Sleeping Beauty was a ghost. Dahlia sighed. All this time they'd been so close, yet had never known it! She slipped over and wrapped her arms around the taller girl's shoulders.

"Laura," she said. "There's a lot we need to talk about. Come with me?"

The new ghost was weak and trembly, and followed Dahlia easily at first. But as they reached the boiler room wall, Laura would go no farther.

"What's the matter?" Dahlia asked, but the girl shook her head so hard her long braids flashed out like a whirligig. There was something about her . . . though she had to be an older teenager, Laura almost seemed younger than Dahlia herself. Did that have to do with having been ghost dust for a century . . . or was it something more?

The boiler room it was, then. Dahlia made herself a little air-cushion, crossed her legs under her, and started talking. Laura didn't react when Dahlia explained to her that she had died. She didn't react to much of anything, actually, and Dahlia started to get a little worried. "What *do* you remember?" she asked gently. "About before?"

Laura looked up at her, blinking. "I died, truly? It is only . . . that it seems like but a few minutes ago that I was telling Mama . . ." She trailed off, and though Dahlia waited patiently, she seemed to have lost her train of thought, drifting from one wall to the other, looking carefully at every chink and crack in the plaster.

"Laura?" Dahlia said.

"My new room was so lovely." Laura's voice was as wispy as her form. She was trailing her finger across the surface of the boiler now. "All the way in the tippy-toppy reaches of the attic. I was so pleased with it and Mama went to an awful lot of trouble having the carpenters prepare it for me. But as soon as I moved in there I knew that it wasn't right."

Something in her tone chilled Dahlia as much as her actual words. She was talking about the room where they had both lived—and died, apparently. What was going on?

"The room was evil, you see. I could tell that right away. But Mama wouldn't listen. She had gone to such expense, she said, and how silly of me not to enjoy it after all of that! I thought perhaps she was right, but oh, the headaches! I cannot begin to describe the pain and weakness I began to feel from the very first night. I even felt . . ." She paused, and suddenly her gaze was sharp, and so incredibly sad. "I even felt at times that I might be losing my mind. But I see now, at last, that this was not the case."

"What . . . what do you mean?"

"There was a presence in the room with me all the time. A lurking evil. I could not see it then but I could sense it, could feel it eroding my mind and working away at my nerves."

Dahlia wanted to cry, not only for what Laura had suffered in her life, but even more for the sad bits of her that were left. She was talking plain crazy.

As Laura idly traced her hand across the boiler, she

abruptly stilled. She turned to face Dahlia again, her index finger pointing at an opening in the ancient machinery. "Here it is," she whispered. "Here is the source of that evil. I felt it when I was . . . alive . . . and I felt it somehow through that long sleep that seemed to go so quickly and yet last forever. Once I was free I chased it all through the small passageways of this house."

"The vents?" Dahlia was confused. What was Laura talking about? "You were moving through the heating vents."

"Look!" Laura leaned in until her ear was up against the narrow opening where she had been pointing. "Listen! Can you hear it? Can you see it?"

Dahlia decided to stop thinking the other ghost was crazy and pay attention to what she was actually saying. She leaned closer, and . . .

"What *is* that?" With her ghost-sight she could clearly see the waves of heat rippling a pale orangey-red. But there was something else, too, underlying the heat. There was a dark purple thread, twining alongside and in between the heat molecules. Something that pulsed with a familiar beat. "No," she whispered.

"Yes," said Laura, reaching her ghost-hands out and separating the thin strand, holding it up like a very sheer scarf, then letting it drop back down with the rest of the heat as it traveled out through the vents and up, up, up into the house.

"Poison?" Dahlia echoed. "But how . . . what . . ." Her eyes traveled to a small, newer inscription tacked onto the side of the ancient boiler: *Machinery should be inspected regularly to ensure that carbon monoxide levels are regular. A leak can raise carbon monoxide to perilous levels, which can lead to health hazards including severe head pain, mood swings, personality disorders, amnesia, and death.*

Carbon monoxide? Could it really be? The thin purple thread seemed to mock her. She thought back to all the news articles they had read. They were cursed, the Silverton family, cursed with . . . what? Strange personality disorders, mysterious debilitating illnesses, memory loss . . . and death. Could it be this horribly simple?

She knew her mother had never cared much for mechanical things. She would never have had someone inspect the heating system, but could so many others before her have been ignorant of such things, all those many years ago? She sighed. Actually, she could very much believe it. And more than that: the house was huge, and she knew for a fact that her mother had kept the heat on very low. The house had terrible insulation, and it was always freezing as the heat escaped through little cracks here and there that would have cost too much to fix and so never were taken care of. In the deepest winter, just about every room had its own space heater, to supplement the weak heating system.

Every room except the attic. Laura's attic room. And her own.

That room was sealed as tight as a drum. Oh! If she closed her eyes, she could see herself now on that fateful last night, slamming the window shut against the winter's cold, her mother turning up the heat just this once because it was so unexpectedly cold, and all those fumes, unseen but deadly, creeping in to fill the empty space.

Dahlia's eyes were shining with tears when she looked up and met Laura's own. "Carbon monoxide poisoning," she said. "That was the problem all along, since the very beginning. Some were cursed to live and grow old with it poisoning their brains little by little. You and I got a huge death dose of it all at once." She reached out a hand toward Laura, who was still pointing at the faulty opening. "This is the curse, right here." A curse that wasn't a curse at all—just human neglect and terrible, terrible ignorance. So much damage had been caused by this one machine, so much harm done.

Closing her hand over Laura's, Dahlia took a deep breath and lifted their palms toward the boiler. The second she made Contact, the air around her started to crackle and shimmer.

Shifting into Clearsight, she gazed through the walls to the outdoors, through the garden, up to the gate and . . . Yes! As she watched, a huge swirly dome leapt into sight, encasing the house. The dome crackled as though with millions of volts of electricity. Then there was a *POOF.*

And the dome disappeared.

The Boundary was gone.

Chapter 26

The Jolly Marzipans were a huge success. Oliver could tell by the way the applause echoed loudly through the house, and by the clink of toppling-over punch glasses as the guests eagerly rushed forward to congratulate Mr. Day on his fine accomplishment. Whether the enthusiasm would have been *quite* so extreme if the punch had been less . . . *punchy* was another story. But still, from his hiding spot at the back of the portrait room Oliver had to admit that Dad's show had been pretty impressive. In his mind he could already see the view-counter on his dad's website skyrocketing after this performance. Maybe even enough to bring that success he'd been chasing for as long as Oliver could remember.

Too bad it was going to come too late for the thing Oliver wanted most in the world.

Meanwhile, with the puppet show over, the guests were starting to move back downstairs. While the show was on,

Rutabartle had been busy too. The partygoers ambled through the hallway and back downstairs, toward the snack table, which Mom had filled with a new round of salmon-cheese puffs, ham will-o-the-wisps, and her specialty, deep-fried stuffed olives. But Oliver lingered back to watch the town official.

Rutabartle had set up a folding table right in the center of the balcony overlooking the gathering hall. Not so far, in fact, from the spot Oliver had recently used for spying. Grinding his teeth a little, Oliver found a new spot, a dark alcove on the other end adjoining the staircase. From there he could watch both the party guests and Rutabartle, who was gathering papers and various other objects into place and clearing his throat noisily. The auction was about to begin, apparently.

But it didn't—not yet. Instead, Rutabartle whipped out a red plastic megaphone and started hollering into it: "Ladies and gentlemen, thank you so very much for coming tonight to attend the grand Silverton Manor Open House!"

Down in the dining room, Oliver could see Mom roll her eyes and huff off toward the kitchen. She must not have liked Rutabartle taking credit for her party any more than Oliver did.

"As you well know, this amazingly fine piece of property, which was not to go on the market until next April, has now astoundingly been made available nearly six months early!"

This was not news to any of the party guests, but still their faces looked doubtful. Despite everything they had seen on their tour tonight, despite Mom and Dad and their normal kids, and despite Rutabartle's many attempts to drum up enthusiasm, people still seemed nervous about putting down money on the manor. And why not? Hadn't they known about the curse for decades—gossiped about it, feared and dreaded it? Oliver's heart lifted a bit. Maybe there was still hope. Maybe no one would bid in Rutabartle's auction, and he would call it off, and their family could stay. Long enough to save up more money, or at least to figure out what to do next.

But the man wasn't finished yet. "I am fully aware of the noxious reputation that has been cast about concerning Silverton Manor. Old trenches deeply dug are not the easiest to clamber out of, so to speak. Therefore, to aid you in your mental transition from uncertainty to appreciation, please enjoy this modest show."

Rutabartle leaned down toward his table and started poking and prodding something. A few seconds later a slim white screen rose out of a machine on the table. Once it was all unfurled, Rutabartle pressed a button and gentle violin music curled around the hall. Words flashed on the screen:

Silverton Manor: A Very Normal Family Home

Oliver's eyes widened. What? The first thing he saw was an image of the whole Day family, standing on the bluff overlooking Silverton Manor. The sun peeped from behind the distant turret spire and the whole house was bathed in liquid gold. For a second, Oliver wanted to smile and lean back in his alcove at the beauty of the scene, but then he snapped back to reality. Where had Rutabartle gotten this footage of their family?

Next, the image shifted to a kitchen scene: the whole family sitting around the table laughing and talking ... though there was an occasional sour look directed toward the camera.

Oliver scanned the downstairs to see his parents' reactions, but Mom still hadn't come back from the kitchen, and now that he thought about it, Dad probably hadn't yet left his puppet room. What were they going to say? Had Rutabartle been filming them secretly?

The next scene was subtitled:

A Wonderful Place for Normal Children to Grow Up.

The image showed JJ chasing each other back and forth in front of the newly planted flowerbeds. This had to be very recent, as the gardeners had only just finished that landscaping. He had to hand it to Rutabartle—it sure did *look* normal ... especially if you didn't know JJ, and if you didn't know the sack they were tossing back and forth was their infamous Bag of Pranks, and if you didn't know that earlier that morning they had booby-trapped the side door with a bowl of bright-green Jell-O.

JJ turned, exchanged a scheming glance, then let out a joint howl. They started running toward the camera, and Oliver could see mischief gleaming in their eyes. The scene quickly shifted to a slow pan of the upstairs hallway, but in that moment, Oliver understood.

He remembered how Rutabartle's sunglasses had always drawn his eye, how they seemed somehow too big, all mirrored and mechanized, and how Rutabartle was always fiddling with them at the oddest times. But . . . not fiddling after all. *Filming.*

Then he thought of that Normalcy Questionnaire he and Poppy had filled out. And the small-print question on the last page: *Do you agree to cooperate in various candid film and photographic shots, to be held at a time of the licensor's choosing, and to be displayed without limitations, in gatherings of no more than seventy-five persons?* He and Poppy had laughed so hard at this question, imagining Rutabartle posing them for family shots on the lawn. And they had checked the box. This was all their fault.

The film ended, and Rutabartle drew in his screen. "Ladies and gentlemen," he said. "I think this film speaks for itself. I will allow you some more time to ponder and discuss the matter among yourselves. I will also add that, in deference to the manor's astonishing history and to show how serious I am about launching a successful auction tonight, I have decided to begin the auction with no floor—yes, ladies and gentlemen, I mean *no* lowest starting bid." A rumble began among the guests. Rutabartle definitely had their attention now. "That is all, my friends. The auction will begin in precisely fifteen minutes. Until then—enjoy your evening!"

Oliver felt sick. How were any of these wealthy buyers going to resist *that* kind of offer? He could already see several ladies turning rapt eyes toward the banisters, with a look he knew all too well: the gleam of ownership. Others had pulled out their phones and were poking furiously at the screens, bringing up numbers and leaning in close to tap out messages or muttering into their headsets. The food and drink was all but forgotten. Right in front of his eyes, Oliver's dream of staying at Silverton Manor officially fizzled and died.

And if he'd thought things couldn't get any worse, they suddenly did. Across the floor downstairs, a door on the end of the hall opened. It closed again, just as quickly, but this time Oliver knew he hadn't been mistaken: Rank Wiley the ghosterminator was loose in the house.

Well, this at least Oliver could do something about. While taking care to stay out of sight of his parents, of course. Dad was still in puppet-land, but Mom was now buzzing on the far side of the room, refilling glasses and circulating like her best idea of a good hostess. Keeping one eye on her back, Oliver darted out of his hiding spot, skulked halfway down the stairs, and dove into another alcove. This was where JJ had been earlier, when they had gooped the party guest, and if he wasn't mistaken . . . Yes! Right there on the floor, stuffed under the small decorative armchair, was their Bag of Pranks.

Ducking farther into the shadows, Oliver poked through the bag. There wasn't much. Except . . . what was Dad's lucky hat doing here? He realized now that Dad hadn't been wearing it during the puppet show, yet everything had gone off without a hitch. Apparently Dad's luck was doing just fine. Still, the hat seeded a plan in Oliver's mind.

Downstairs, Wiley was on the move, skulking through the party like a rhinoceros in a flock of flamingos. No one seemed to notice him, which was the weirdest thing ever since he had a big white dish towel draped over his shoulder. And peeping out of the towel was the telltale neon-orange glow of the Aspirator.

Oliver remembered how the ghostly woman, Mrs. Tibbs, had spoken from inside the little container—just like a real person. And living or not, she *was* real. What would it be like to be trapped in a box, being carted off somewhere to be dissected and analyzed? Oliver sure wouldn't want that to happen to him after he died.

Wiley had to be stopped.

A crazy idea shot into his mind. It was risky, but right now, it was all he had. Dad's hat would come in handy sooner than he'd expected. Pushing it on his head and tugging the brim over his eyes, he barreled down the stairs and into the mass of guests. Wiley was just up ahead . . . not too much farther. Oliver sped up. He pushed past a twiggy-thin woman and heard a gurgle and splash followed by a refined shriek. He ducked low under two outstretched hands being shaken in welcome. He heard behind him, faintly, "Arthur? Is that you, darling? Did you get any—"

And there was Wiley. Oliver leaped, landing on Wiley in a full-body tackle that sent them both sprawling across a mercifully empty stretch of floor. At the same time, Oliver raised his head and yelled as loud as he could: "Ghost! There's a ghost in the house!" He turned toward Wiley, who was picking himself up off the floor and said, looking right into his eyes: "The house is *still* haunted."

Chapter 27

Dahlia couldn't believe it—the Boundary was gone. *Gone!* Years and years she'd been waiting for this moment, and now she hardly knew what to do first. Pumping one fist high into the air, she corkscrewed into a plume of whirling ghost-matter and shot straight up. She rocketed through the roof and in a second skimmed through the cool misty clouds, startling a bird and, a few seconds later, sluicing through the far wing of a jetliner. She flew faster than she ever had before, bouncing down on one rooftop, swinging from a distant bell tower, dropping down into the ocean—*the ocean! Deep, blue, rippling water with real live fish everywhere*—before rising up like an invisible mermaid to collapse on some yellow-sand beach with a happy sigh.

She was free! Right now she, Dahlia Silverton, was lying on a beach somewhere miles and miles away from Silverton Manor—so far she didn't even have a clue where she was. She laughed out loud, and giggled at the way the sound was swallowed up in the wide open space. The sunlight was warm, so unlike anything she'd seen in the tree-lined clearing back home.

Life was good.

Wait! It was not just warmer here, but brighter too. Dahlia opened her eyes and squinted across the beach. About a hundred feet across the water, light was gathering into a glimmering pulse-point. It was stretching out into . . . a door? Yes. The door opened and a serious-looking man stepped through, obviously a ghost from the way his sharply defined edges stood out against the see-through swath of the living ocean.

As the man approached, he pulled a long stick-like device from his shirt pocket, much like the one Mrs. Tibbs had used the first day Dahlia met her. He opened it up and prodded the virtual screen. He raised an eyebrow. "Dahlia Silverton?" he intoned.

"Yes?" she squeaked, sitting up to attention.

"Rupert Milton," the man said. "I'm pleased to make your acquaintance. May I ask what brings you . . . here?" He looked around himself distastefully. "Is this your Passing Point?"

"Where I died, you mean? Here? Oh no! I just went on a quick joyride. I was so happy to be able to leave my Boundary, you see. Have you come to greet me? Are you the welcoming committee?" Dahlia couldn't wait to see what came next. It felt like she'd been waiting for this moment forever.

But Milton frowned. "Hmm. It's somewhat irregular, but easily remedied. If you'll come over here?"

Dahlia wasn't sure what he meant, but zipped over to hover with him next to the portal.

"Place a hand here, if you please," Milton explained. "We'll have this rectified in no time. Procedure must be followed, you see. Crossing over should happen from the correct location, or it creates an absolutely atrocious mountain of paperwork! Forms and permissions that you couldn't begin to imagine."

Dahlia rested a hand on the side of the portal. There was a gushing noise like a faucet on full blast, except it wasn't water but the world sucking by around them, while the door and Milton and Dahlia stayed steady. In three or four seconds the world slowed again and they were standing by the front gate of Silverton Manor. The door was placed so that it overlaid the front manor gate exactly. Dahlia was standing just inside the property—at the very spot, in fact, where she had spent so many long hours trying to cross over. A feeling of satisfaction welled up inside her.

"Well now," Milton said, looking pleased to have so easily righted things. He leaned toward Dahlia and held up his device. "Place your thumb here to begin the process."

Dahlia saw her name printed neatly on the screen, with a blue-outlined box labeled IDENTIFICATION. She pressed her thumb firmly in the spot. The device hummed lightly, then glowed bright green.

"Excellent," said Milton. "Now the next step—"

"Dahlia?" came a sudden voice, echoing through space.

Dahlia turned around. "Oh!" she cried. In her excitement at being free, she'd forgotten all about the other ghost. "Oh, Mr. Milton. This is Laura Silverton, an ancestor of mine. Are you here to collect her too? She's been trapped in the manor even longer than I have. In an upstairs attic room, and quite unconscious! Can you imagine?"

Laura still looked a bit wispy as she came to hover next to Dahlia, but her gaze was clear and she didn't seem nearly as wild-eyed as before. Dahlia hoped that, whatever damage had led to her death—some of which apparently still affected her—she would be able to fully recover from it now that things were back to normal. If anyone needed to cross over, Laura Silverton did.

But Milton was frowning at his screen. "A joint crossing over? Most irregular! Has the proper paperwork been filed? Have the correct procedures been met? I cannot be expected to . . ."

"Mr. Milton, surely you have some sort of, er, missing persons database? Can't you just look her up? The name is Laura Silverton," Dahlia repeated slowly. Mrs. Tibbs had mentioned paperwork and red tape, but really!

Milton sputtered. "Well, I suppose so, but—" He cocked his head to the side. "Who was the Liberator on this case? That's what I would like to know."

Dahlia's eyes widened. "Mrs. Tibbs!" she said. "I can't believe

I didn't tell you already. She's trapped! Some ghosterminating guy has imprisoned her in an ironite container and she can't get out. You need to do something to help her!"

Milton's eyebrows nearly shot off the top of his face. "Elizabeth Tibbs has been Manifesting to the Living?"

"No!" Dahlia exclaimed. "She never did. Not once. But she's trapped anyway. You have to rescue her!"

Milton sighed. "Very well. I will file a report. But can we return to the subject at hand? You mentioned a second Liberation. Was Elizabeth Tibbs involved in this subject's case also?"

"Oh, no!" Laura gushed. "Dahlia did everything! She freed me from my prison, awoke me from my long-dormant state, and helped me to regain my past. I did not even know I was dead until she came!"

Milton turned his eyes toward Dahlia, who quickly stammered. "Um, well, I didn't exactly..." Somehow she had a feeling that a ghost of this ilk would not be impressed by her do-it-yourself approach to ghosting. "Things just sort of... came together. You know? Things do, sometimes."

Milton's forehead wrinkled. "Well, I shall need to file a report with the proper authorities. A number of reports, in fact. The matter warrants further investigation, it seems to me. Be that as it may, all does seem to be in order for you to cross over, and I've located your record in the Circular. Another misfiling, it would appear." He sniffed. "If you'll place your print right here, miss, we can hold the Crossing at the same time."

Laura's hand shook a little as she put her thumbprint onto

the screen. She seemed about to faint with excitement. Dahlia knew exactly how she felt. And yet . . . a thought had started to grow inside Dahlia, something important, something she didn't really want to think about but was suddenly having a very hard time putting aside. "What happens next?" she blurted out. "We cross over, and then what? Can we go anywhere after that?"

Milton let out a bark of laughter, which sent him into an immediate choking fit, as if that idea was so ludicrous he could hardly stand it. "Anywhere you want? My dear child, what kind of outfit is it that you think we are running here?" He snorted. "Nothing of the sort. You will be given the full Rulebook as soon as the Crossing is completed, but you should count on at least fifteen day-cycles to complete your initial Orientation, and then you can begin attending seminars to determine your eventual career disposition."

Dahlia came back to reality with a sharp thud. In all the excitement of clearing the Boundary, she'd put the Day family and their living world completely out of her mind. But now she thought of what was going on in Silverton Manor while she was gallivanting around the ghostly planes. She'd fixed the curse for herself and Laura, but what about the Days? The carbon monoxide leak was still going on, and no one knew a thing about it!

"Step here, please, Miss Laura Silverton. Right this way."

"Mr. Milton," Dahlia said. "Could you wait here for about . . . oh, half an hour, maybe? An hour at the most. I have one quick thing to take care of before I cross over."

Milton looked aghast. "Absolutely not! That is not the way the procedure works. The virtual paper trail has been set in motion, identification ascertained, and the subject must cross over within the next quarter hour. It is the way things are done."

"But I can't do that! Don't you see? The Day children are in danger. They might die if I don't help them!" The idea flitted through her mind that they would then be ghosts—like her!—but just as quickly she dismissed it. It was most definitely not their time. And . . . time was something that they now had very little of. How long had she spent jetting around the world and conversing with bureaucrats?

"Miss Dahlia Silverton," said Milton coldly. "I don't think you understand how Spectral Investigative Council operates. We are here to ensure the process runs as smoothly as it ought. You *must* cross over now, or you will be tagged as a No Cross."

Dahlia turned away slightly and focused her Clearsight through the house. The boiler glowed a dull purple and she could see the tendrils of poisoned air snaking up through the vents, trickling into each room of the house . . . and pumping thick and heavy into the tightly sealed attic room, where Poppy, Joe, and Junie slept soundly. Too soundly. She could already see the dull-purple fumes scratching away at the edges of their auras. She had to get back there, fast.

And what about Mrs. Tibbs, still stuck in the Aspirator? Milton was going to "file a report," and Dahlia had a good idea of how long something like *that* would take. Far, far too long to be any good to anybody, most especially Mrs. Tibbs. Meanwhile, Wiley was loose in the house, and Dahlia would not be at all surprised if he found a way to get the canister back.

There was only one decision she could make.

"I'm sorry," she said. "I can't cross over."

"This is unheard of!" the official thundered. "Your afterlife will be forever marred by this decision, girl. A Re-Crossing can take years of paperwork filing and legalities, with the outcome uncertain. Some No-Cross parties have been incarcerated and none—*not a single one*—has ever gone on to a productive or influential career. Would you really trade any possibility of future freedom for these . . . living folks?"

Dahlia looked at the glowering official, then at Laura's hopeful face. She opened her mouth.

And then a voice came plaintively through the portal. "Dahlia? My dear, is that you?" A face shimmered just on the other side of the door—a face as young and fresh as in Dahlia's years-ago memory.

"Mama," she whispered, a lump rising in her throat.

"Now, now, Mrs. Silverton," huffed Milton. "All in due time, this is not correct procedure!"

Dahlia felt her bones wilting like flower stems. Her mother wanted her—knew her—was calling her! And yet . . .

She looked back toward Silverton Manor, walls all aglow where they had once held nothing but forbidding gloom. She'd wanted to leave, yes. *Needed* to, even. And now, more than ever, she had a reason to leave, somewhere to go. Someone to belong to again. But if leaving meant deserting those she had come to care about, failing them right when they needed her most—well, how could she live with herself after that?

"I'm sorry, Mr. Milton," she said, slowly but firmly. "But I have to stay." She turned and locked eyes with her mother. "There are people who need me here. I'll come just as soon as I can." She waited a fraction of a second, until she saw her mother's tiny nod, and then she gave Laura's hand a squeeze and she was off.

Dahlia shot straight up to the attic, bursting through the wall and looking wildly around. Poppy was on the floor, half-on and half-off a narrow mat. The twins were sprawled on her bed, swathed in bedding. All three were sound asleep.

The window was tightly shut, and even in her ghost form Dahlia could feel the curls of carbon monoxide wrapping around her, reminding her in tiny chokes and gasps how her spirit had felt when she had died at their hands, so many years ago. She put a hand on either side of her head and willed herself to concentrate. She needed to get someone to help the kids. But first, she had to find a way to dilute the deadly gas.

Desperately, she jutted her hand into the Seesaw. But the old device stayed as dead and quiet as before. Blast that broken machine! If only she were able to interact with the living world. She remembered how Mrs. Tibbs had easily plucked those library books off the shelf, the way she'd turned the pages of the family Bible. Dahlia hadn't been able to muster the same sort of success, but she had to try.

She rushed over to Poppy, grabbed the girl's shoulders ... but her hands slid right through to the bed. She poked the twins, but only succeeded in riffling the cloth on their pajamas. Dahlia ground her teeth, focused all her energy, and yelled. Nothing—not a sound crossed over to the living world.

Gazing frantically around the room, she caught sight of the old, yellowed calendar. *The Star Lover's Guide to 1954.* Her calendar, so many years ago. Her eyes widened as she thought of her own makeshift calendars, her star charts, carved into the tree out on the property. She'd worked on those for hours, for days, carving her heart and soul into the bark of that tree. She *could* affect the living world. She just had to find the right medium.

Dahlia steadied herself, forced her mind to work logically through the options. Around her, the air itself glowed a virulent purple, wisps pushing at the window as though looking for a way out.

The window? Maybe.

Dahlia shot toward the glass, bringing herself up short in front of it. She could make herself kneel lightly on the wooden chest; it was a start. Raising her fist, she punched the glass as hard as she could. Her fist passed straight through. Over and over she hit at the glass—tried to purge her mind of emotion, tried to figure, tried to *connect.* Nothing worked.

She looked down. The telescope sat on the floor next to

the chest, and her mind pulsed with what it had meant to her, both in her former life and as her Anchor.

And then she thought: Why not that?

Maybe she couldn't break through objects, but she could grasp them. She could touch them. Maybe that would be enough.

Moving very slowly, Dahlia opened her fingers and closed them around the end of the telescope. One inch at a time—making sure she had a solid hold, emptying her mind of everything but the stars, the sky, the need to accomplish this one simple task—she strained and lifted.

It worked! She was carrying the telescope.

She pulled it back from the window. She closed her eyes, then opened them, focusing her willpower even more sharply. She drew back, then thrust with all her might. The telescope shot forward—and crashed through the window, toppling out and down to the garden below.

Chapter 28

Oliver caught his breath as, at the word *GHOST*, the entire hall seemed to freeze. Then a ripple went through the crowd, followed by a nervous tittering. Someone started clapping, and pretty soon the whole room was roaring enthusiastically.

"Simply fabulous!"

"What a fine spooky touch—delicious irony!"

"Without a doubt the best party of the year."

Oliver slumped in place. Nothing was going right. What more could he do? The partygoers had returned to their sipping and munching and, worse, Oliver could see Mom stuck behind two very large guests but glaring in his direction. She had obviously seen through his Dad disguise and was on her way over to nab him.

A hand grasped his arm, and Oliver jumped. "Good call, young man," Wiley said confidentially. "An audacious move, to be sure, but desperate times and all that. You caught me just in time and I want you to know that I'm *on the case*. That nasty vermin will not escape my ghosterminator's reach—I am Rank T. Wiley, and the *T* stands for *Tenacious!*"

Wiley was off like a shot, and Oliver wished he could fall through the floor and disappear. Now Wiley was going to pull out his machines and start hunting Dahlia. Could things possibly get any worse?

"Ladies and gentlemen! That moment you have been waiting for so patiently has finally arrived. It is time to auction off Silverton Manor!"

Apparently it could.

Amid the deafening applause, Oliver could hear his mother's voice getting nearer. He scanned the room for Wiley, but the ghosterminator had disappeared. He would have to hunt him down pretty soon, but there was one thing he needed to do first. Ducking under an arm, Oliver dove through the crowd. He scooted all the way to the back of the room, where he parked himself in front of a window. The pane was steamy from heat bubbling up out of a vent that sat just below it. Oliver pulled his father's hat lower over his eyes, satisfied to see Mom heading in the opposite direction. He just had to stay hidden for a few minutes longer.

Reaching into his pocket, he pulled out a scrap of paper. He looked at the number written there. No way would it ever be enough. But it was the only thing left to do. Oliver settled back and waited for Rutabartle to finish his introductory speech. The man described the house from top to bottom, listed all its virtues, and with every glowing word Oliver felt himself sink a little lower.

"And now, ladies and gentlemen—give me your best offers," Rutabartle bellowed, pounding the folding table with a real wooden gavel, which made the scrawny metal legs skitter across the floor.

Oliver cleared his throat, trying to make his voice sound extra gruff and low, and as much like his dad as possible. With all the noise and the bustle, surely this would work. Anyway, he had his father's hat on. "Three hundred and ninety-four dollars!" he yelled across the room. He didn't mention the twenty-one cents, because that would sound ridiculous.

It was kind of ridiculous already, he was well aware.

There was a stunned silence. The hall had been noisy enough that most people weren't sure where the opening bid had come from but, pulling his hat down farther in front of his face, Oliver waved his hand at Rutabartle, who looked confused but nodded his head in reluctant acceptance.

"An opening bid from Mr. Arthur Day. A very *modest* bid, but"—he waved his hand grandly—"I have said there is no floor, and you see that I am a man of my word!" He laughed comfortably, then narrowed his eyes. "Now, who else is going to offer for this jewel of an estate?"

"Ten thousand dollars!" came a piercing cry from across the room.

"Mrs. Elvira Lawson, now we are starting to bid in earnest," purred Rutabartle. "Ten thousand dollars it is, and who will make it twenty? Mr. Stein? Certainly. Now I'm looking at thirty thousand—a nice healthy jump, yes?"

Oliver's heart sank. He thought about the money his dad hoped to make on his new Jolly Marzipan show. Would it be enough? Could Oliver maybe raise his bid using money they didn't have yet but would soon? Mom and Dad would just deny the bid, of course, so it wouldn't be much use.

Then a light *ping* caught his ear. He turned in time to see a rosemary-parmesan cracker drop to the floor. Oliver picked it up with a frown. Another cracker hit him in the forehead. He turned quickly and saw, right in the corner next to him, a handful of olives rise from a small bowl and begin juggling in the empty air, shimmying toward the window.

Oliver grinned. Dahlia, of course! As the olives reached the pane, he held out his hand and they fell to his palm in a neat row. He popped them into his mouth. Then he looked at the window and his eyes widened. Letters were forming on the steamy pane. Turning quickly to block the view from any passersby, Oliver watched a message appear: "Danger—kids—hurry!"

"Upstairs?" he whispered urgently. "They're in danger right now?" He wanted to dash right off, but he could see more words forming below the others. "Carbon monoxide caused my death. Still leaking. GO!"

Oliver went. He paused only one moment at the back door, looking back over to the hall and Rutabartle poised high on his vantage point, yelling, "One hundred and fifteen thousand—and who will raise me to one thirty?"

With a silent good-bye to his dreams, Oliver dashed through the door toward the back stairs and raced up them two at a time. He tore down the hall and up the next flight of stairs, his heart pounding. Suddenly his need to live in Silverton Manor seemed so small. How had that become the most important thing in his life? How could anything be more important than his brother and sisters? JJ with their ridiculous pranks that kept life from ever getting boring. And Poppy—who had somehow, over the last two weeks, turned into the coolest sister ever. Had he ever bothered to tell her that?

Clearing the last steps, Oliver slammed the attic door open. The noise was loud and explosive, but none of the kids moved. The room was just as he'd left it—except for shards of glass strewn across the floor by the window, which had a jagged hole in it. Carbon monoxide, Dahlia had written. Well, wasn't that impossible to see or smell? And why weren't Poppy and JJ moving? Someone—Dahlia, apparently—had punched through the glass, and they hadn't even woken up.

Oliver dropped to his knees next to Poppy, who was the closest to the door, and began to shake her. "Wake up!" he yelled. "Poppy, wake up!"

Poppy was groggy but sat up slowly. Her eyes were unfocused. "Wha . . . ?" she mumbled. "What's . . . going on?"

Oliver yanked her by the arm and Poppy squeaked. "Wake up!" he yelled. "Poppy, wake up!"

He half-pulled, half-dragged her to the landing. "What's going on? My head feels like a marshmallow." Her voice was muddled and thick.

Oliver looked at her, stick-skinny and shivering on the floor. "You're gonna be okay now," he said. "And actually, I think you're better than okay." He punched her lightly in the arm. "Really. Now I've got to run back and get the twins, all right? They're still in danger."

He left her scrambling to her feet and dashed back into the room.

He shook Junie first, but she just lolled in his arms. He looked up with horror at the air vent, directly above the bed. Her small body was already taken over by the poison. No! He grabbed her under one arm and tried to get Joe with the other, but Junie slipped out of his hands. He couldn't hold them both at once. But he couldn't leave either of them here for another moment.

All at once, he saw the bed next to him dip slightly, as though somebody invisible was sitting on it. Joe rose a little in the air—cradled in invisible arms. Oliver felt relief swell inside him. Dahlia was there. "We have to get them downstairs," he said. "They're unconscious or something—they were right underneath the vent where the carbon monoxide was coming out. It can't be too late! We need an ambulance. We have to get them to Mom and Dad."

As if in reply, Joe was pressed into a ball and lifted up into the air. Oliver shouldered Junie and jumped off the bed, starting in a run for the attic stairs. Poppy was standing there waiting, her legs still trembling, eyes wide and scared. "What's going on, Oliver?" she said.

"Come on, tagalong," Oliver said. "Let's do this together."

It was time to break up the party.

Chapter 29

Dahlia felt a trickle of sweat starting between her shoulder blades. She had never concentrated so hard in her life. It was one thing to sit on a branch, to rub words onto steamed-up glass—even to pick up a telescope for a few seconds and punch it through a window. But to carry a real living child down three flights of stairs, at top speed? This was entirely different. She forced her arms into steel bars, and glided a few feet off the ground to keep the journey as smooth as possible. Over and over she reminded herself, *Do not ghost through anything!* The last thing she wanted was to slip through a chair or potted plant, and end up with the poor kid splatted on the floor on the other side.

"Come on," Oliver whispered, looking back over his shoulder at her. "Poppy and I will go run ahead and warn them, okay? Everyone's down in the gathering hall. Hurry!"

With that, he dashed off, with Poppy following weakly

along behind him. She still looked befuddled, but the more she walked, the stronger she seemed. The girl would be all right.

Dahlia knew that she herself couldn't keep up. With everything she had to concentrate on, the best she could manage was a slow creep down the stairs. She wouldn't be fast, but she would get there.

Little Joe, on the other hand . . . In her arms, his face was pale. His chest was rising and falling, but so very faintly. Dahlia's ghost sight couldn't exactly see all the way through a living body, but certain systems were visible. And Joe's systems were definitely not doing all that they should. Dahlia clenched her arms tighter and sped down to the last flight of steps. Ahead was the hum of voices, the bustle of swishing feet and the clink of glasses. A loud voice—it sounded like that town official, the one with the name like a bad-tasting vegetable— boomed out over a megaphone: "And it's a wrap, folks! Silverton Manor has been SOLD to the eminent Mrs. Poitiers in the far corner. My congratu—"

And then, a collective gasp and Oliver's voice raised loud and clear: "Help! There's been a carbon monoxide leak upstairs. Someone call 911!"

She could feel Joe slipping through her arms, but she rushed on faster. The downstairs hall was a whirl of noise and commotion—people shuffling, voices raised in mild alarm, and the slight crackle of the megaphone and a voice trying to be heard over the noise. Dahlia came around the corner to the

top of the stairs, and she knew she was close to dropping Joe.
The downstairs was a buzz of activity, and she couldn't see
Oliver or Poppy or their parents anywhere. She had to get the
little boy to safety! Lowering her burden quickly to the ground,
she shifted him into a better position, scooted one arm under
his back and the other under his behind, closed her eyes for
maximum concentration, and lifted.

The crowds ahead parted, and she could see Poppy and
Oliver standing over Junie, who lay on some cushions on the
floor. His parents hovered in close. Then Mrs. Day clapped her
hands to her chest. "Joe!" she shrieked. "Where's my Joey?"

Oliver turned in Dahlia's direction, and his eyes widened.
He started shaking his head frantically, like in all the rush he'd
forgotten something very important.

Mr. and Mrs. Day turned to follow his gaze. Their mouths
dropped all the way open and their faces went sheet-white.
One by one, the guests turned to look in her direction, and she
suddenly knew what they were seeing: a very little boy hanging suspended in the air, unconscious, drifting across the room
with no visible means of support.

Oops.

Dahlia sped up. She would get the boy to Oliver, put him
down on the floor, and leave. What, would they rather she'd
left him in the attic?

The crowd parted like falling dominoes. A whisper started
up next to Dahlia and whizzed around the hall: *Spirits! The*

child is possessed—he's moving under a foreign power! Is there really nothing holding him up? And, rising above everything else: *Ghosts! Silverton Manor really is haunted!*

The screaming started next, a high-pitched wailing howl that went on and on. Then a voice cut through the ruckus, a voice as chilly as the dark night outside: "Step aside, everyone. Let the experts take over. Everything's going to be all right."

Any remaining bystanders pulled themselves farther out of the way and, into the empty spot marched Rank Wiley, goggles over his eyes, his long, thin Spectrometer in hand, pointing right at Dahlia.

Dahlia's heart started pounding in her chest, and she could feel Joe starting to slip again. What could she do? She couldn't get away when she was holding the little boy, and she didn't want to drop him, either. She was hovering about six feet off the ground, and could see the floor below her feet. If she set Joe down right now, she could make a quick getaway—zip right through these people and be gone for good. Joe would probably be all right.

But what if he wasn't? She could feel the palpable panic around her, and could see the bleary looks in the eyes of the partygoers. Even now people were shoving and pushing; the little space around her was kept open only for knowing that a *ghost* was trapped inside it.

Smash! A wineglass went hurtling across the room and crunched on the ground at Dahlia's feet. That settled it. Dahlia shot higher into the air, above the guests' heads. She had to get to the cushioned area where the Days were gathered. She'd leave Joe there and then make a dash for safety.

The screeching rose as Dahlia swirled around the chandelier.

"Come back here, dread specter of the deep!" intoned Wiley. He had put away the Spectrometer and lifted up the goggles, apparently realizing he didn't need a device to track her since she was holding Joe. But would he really spray her when she was holding a kid? Dahlia sneaked a look over her shoulder at Wiley's determined face.

Oh, yes. No doubt about that.

Dahlia circled the far side of the chandelier, dodged a pair of elderly biddies, and finally—*finally!*—came down near the Day family.

"Right here," Oliver whispered, scooting over. "Now you have to go! I'm so sorry about Wiley . . ."

Dahlia set Joe down, stroked his forehead lovingly. The boy's eyes fluttered open. He was only half-conscious, Dahlia could tell, and for a moment, his form stuttered between looking see-through and fully formed. Joe looked right at Dahlia, seeing her, and smiled. He blinked twice and opened his eyes again, fully see-through once more to Dahlia, and jabbed the still-unconscious Junie in the ribs. "Hey, move over, dummy! You're using all the cushions!"

Junie grumbled and poked him back, and Dahlia let out a long sigh. They would be okay. The twins were safe.

From the back of the hall someone yelled. "The ambulance will be here in two minutes!"

And then a quieter voice behind Dahlia: "Do not move a muscle, ghoul. I have you in my sights, and this time you're not getting away."

Chapter 30

Oliver's relief at seeing Joe and Junie open their eyes and start squabbling was short-lived. Rank Wiley was clearly on the warpath, and as far as Oliver could tell, he had Dahlia trapped. Wiley pressed the button on his Aspirator. The phoaming mechanism started to warm up. The pilot light came on, tracing a red pattern in the air and outlining Dahlia's form like a 3-D Etch A Sketch image hanging in the air ahead of him.

"Do not move!" Wiley hissed. "It will be far more painful for you to be in motion, and at this point there is no possible escape."

"Wait!" Oliver yelled at Wiley. *Hurry up and escape!* he thought at Dahlia. But instead, to his horror, he saw Dahlia's outlined form stop in midjump and glance at him expectantly. She thought he was talking to her.

The pilot light coming from the Aspirator turned green. *No!*

Dahlia finally started to move, but it was obvious she would be too late. With no clear plan in mind, Oliver dove past Dahlia and tackled Wiley.

Wiley tumbled backward, but didn't let go of the Aspirator. Roaring in frustration, the ghosterminator aimed the nozzle over Oliver's shoulder. Oliver threw his weight on the offending bag, but not soon enough. With a triumphant crow, Wiley jabbed the ON button so hard that Oliver winced. Wiley was accomplishing his mission and wanted everyone in the room to know it.

The machine started to gurgle. Oliver could see the power revving up and knew the phoam was starting to churn inside the device. The belly of the backpack squirmed faintly. There was a ghost inside there already, Oliver knew. Mrs. Tibbs. He couldn't let Dahlia share her fate. But what could he do? Pinpricks of phoam were popping out of the nozzle. There were just seconds left.

In desperation, he looked over to Poppy, who was flopped weakly on the floor. Her body was still limp from her carbon monoxide poisoning, but her eyes were crackling. She was making weak gestures. Trying to tell him something. But what?

He frowned at her. "The twins!" she called over the hubbub. "What would JJ do?"

Oliver froze as his eyes fell on JJ who sat watching, eyes wide. Of course! He didn't have their Bag of Pranks handy, but . . . maybe he could make do. With a grin for Poppy he leaned over and, quick as a flash, grabbed a soft dinner roll filled with egg salad off a nearby tray. He stuffed the roll into the nozzle of the Aspirator.

The machine stuttered, and Wiley turned his head to look at Oliver, then down at the body of his machine. "What did you do?" the man growled.

Oliver turned so his body hid the nozzle from Wiley's sight. He shoved the roll farther up into the spout—now pushing, he could tell, against the force of the gathering phoam.

Poppy cheered. "Another!" she squeaked.

Oliver quickly grabbed a second roll and shoved it in after the first.

He scrambled back, breathing hard, while Wiley shook the Aspirator, still unsure what had happened while his view was obstructed, wondering why the phoam wasn't coming out yet. With Joe down, Oliver couldn't tell where Dahlia was anymore. He wondered if she'd escaped, or if she was lurking somewhere nearby, watching to see what would happen.

And what *would* happen? The machine was starting to steam, and Wiley was thumbing the button, an increasing look of panic in his eyes. Oliver started to laugh. Had Wiley really pushed the button so hard he'd broken it? Well then, they made a good team.

But the Aspirator wasn't finished. More steam was rising from the motor, and Oliver yelled, "Get back, everybody!" He

scooted over and pulled JJ and Poppy aside. Gawking partygoers scrambled out of the way.

And then—

—the Aspirator imploded. It didn't spiral outward but
burst in on itself in a puff of black smoke. Black smoke . . .
tinged with a pale-green powder. A second later, there was
another explosion, the kind of explosion you'd get if you let a
vacuum cleaner loose in a flour factory.

Pale-green, powdery phoam—blended with yellowish
clumps of egg salad—erupted from the Aspirator's sack like
a giant sneeze, coating all the bystanders. Maybe that's why it
took a few seconds for people to notice what Oliver saw immediately. At the heart of the eruption, something thin and wispy
lay curled up in the tattered remains of the Aspirator. Something which, still caked in goop, slowly stretched out into the
shape of—a tall, wiry woman wearing a giant straw hat, a paisley carpetbag tucked firmly under her arm.

A minute later the first guest saw the phoam-encrusted
ghost, which was now beginning, slowly and steadily, to glow.
If they had needed any further confirmation that the house
was haunted, this was it. The party turned into a stampede as
the guests ran screaming for the nearest exit.

Wiley dropped to the floor in the ruins of his Aspirator.

Rutabartle, still wielding his megaphone, called out,
"Please wait, Mrs. Poitiers! I need your signature right here to
confirm your bid!"

"Not on your life," shrieked the woman from the far side of the hall. "I wouldn't live in this house if you paid me! Consider my bid retracted."

There was a loud *BANG* as the front door burst open. "Police! Where is the emergency?"

A half dozen uniformed officers pushed into the room. Two of them bent down and started examining Junie and Joe. A third began speaking with Mom and Dad. "Carbon monoxide poisoning, you say? And you didn't have any alarms installed?"

Oliver seized his chance. "It was him!" he yelled, pointing at the distracted Wiley, who was pressing the edges of his ruptured bag together, as though hoping it would magically repair itself. "He was pretending to be a handyman. He's been lying this whole time!"

Mom's eyes widened and swung to Wiley's face. "You!" she exclaimed, taking in the ghosterminating equipment. "Do you mean to say you have been here under false pretenses, pretending to work and *living in our house* while secretly conducting a hunt for *ghosts*?"

Oliver frowned at the floor. Mom didn't even seem to remember all those times he'd tried to warn her about this creep. But when he glanced back up she was staring right at him. "I guess some of us take longer than others to see what's right in front of our noses," she said, with a smile that promised pancakes every day for a week and maybe even an extra hour of nighttime TV. Oliver saw Poppy doing a mini-Snoopy dance over in her corner.

A tall policeman stepped up to the beaten ghosterminator and cleared his throat. "I think you'll need to come with us, Mister . . . ?"

"Rank T. Wiley," Oliver put in helpfully. "And the *T* stands for *Terminated.*"

Then he settled back to fully enjoy the chaos.

Chapter 31

I still would have liked to say good-bye," Dahlia said from her perch high up in the oak tree. It had taken hours for the household to settle down the night before, but things were finally getting back to normal. Or at least as normal as the Day family would ever get.

Poised on the branch next to her, Mrs. Tibbs harrumphed. "Tut-tut, my gregarious griddlecake, I'm certain that you do! From everything you've told me, you've been leaning on the Ghouncil's rules like an overworked bookend. What they don't know won't hurt them, I suppose—but one can never be too careful." Mrs. Tibbs lowered her voice and leaned in closer to Dahlia. "You do *not* want to get on the bad side of the Ghouncil, my dear. If they should find out about your crimes—"

"My *crimes!*" Dahlia exploded. "I saved the lives of a bunch of living kids, and—well, together with Oliver—helped rescue *you*, Mrs. Tibbs."

"And don't think I'm not grateful," the Liberator said quickly, reaching out to grasp her hand. "Being in that dark place . . ." She shuddered. "Truly, I am in your debt—quite to the limit! But you know the Ghouncil will not see it that way. They will, in their own fashion, completely overlook any great accomplishments in favor of a few insignificant broken rules."

Dahlia pursed her lips into a pout.

"Nevertheless, it's icing off the cake at this point, since they clearly have no idea of your transgressions. But don't tempt them. Keep away from the Day family, that's my advice."

"At least they will be able to stay in the house," said Dahlia, brightening. She wasn't sure exactly what had happened with the auction, but after the ghostly hullabaloo, all the bidders had angrily withdrawn their bids on the house. All except for the very first recorded bidder—Mr. Arthur Day. Mr. Day had at first protested his involvement, but Dahlia thought she saw Oliver kick his father under the table, hard, and Mr. Day had nodded abruptly and said that it was a rather good deal for this old place and he was definitely on board. Rutabartle had bluffed and blustered, but every guest in attendance was ready to swear that he had promised a no-floor auction. With every other sum withdrawn, the Day family had bought Silverton Manor for a whopping $394.

A series of chimes went off, and Mrs. Tibbs's hat began to vibrate. "Good gracious!" she exclaimed, feeling around the crown of her head until she pulled out her Pin, popping it open with a jaunty crack. "Ah, duty calls: it appears I have been given a new assignment. Greater Mongolia! Good heavens, that's quite a trek."

"I think Liberating must be a glorious life," said Dahlia, a little wistfully. She hadn't told Mrs. Tibbs everything that had happened with the Ghouncil, and how she had missed her chance to cross over. It had been worth the trade, she told herself firmly, looking at the happy faces of the little twins as they bounded out of the front door, beach shovels in hand, and started to tunnel into the flowerbeds.

"That it is! Oh, that it is. I don't wonder if you might find yourself considering such a profession yourself, once you've gone through your training."

"Perhaps," said Dahlia, with forced brightness. What *was* she going to do now? She couldn't cross over, she couldn't interact with the Day family . . . what was left for her?

"Shall we move on together then?" Mrs. Tibbs asked, rising off the branch and dusting off her coat. Dahlia could tell she was eager to get on to her next adventure. "You must be excited to cross over."

"Oh, you go on ahead," said Dahlia quickly. "I have a few things to finish up here."

Mrs. Tibbs cocked her head like she suspected there was something Dahlia wasn't telling her. Then she reached out to squeeze her hand. "You do what you must, my glowing ghostlette. For my part, if there is ever anything I can do for you . . ." She reached a hand into her bag and fished around for a few moments, then pulled out the ornate pocket watch.

She stroked it lovingly for a moment, then stretched out the long gold chain and hung the watch around Dahlia's neck.

"Mrs. Tibbs!" Dahlia exclaimed. "That belonged to your husband."

"That it did, my girl, and my Charley is just as important to me as ever. But I've got other ways to remember him. He's safe and sound right *here*, and *here*." She motioned to her head and her heart in turn. "If there's one thing I've seen throughout this adventure, it's that holding too tightly to the past can hook a body right out of the present."

Dahlia looked down at the watch. "Thank you," she said.

"That way," said Mrs. Tibbs, "you can tell what time it is no matter where you are. And this little token will keep us connected even though we're far apart." She shuddered. "Mongolia! What is the world coming to? But my dear—if ever you need me, you give me a holler, and I'll be back in a flash. All right?"

Dahlia nodded and felt her eyes grow suddenly misty. Impulsively, she leaned forward and wrapped her arms around Mrs. Tibbs. "Thank you," she said. "I'll miss you."

"As will I," Mrs. Tibbs said gravely. She rose in the air, hovered for a second, then took off like a shot.

A gentle breeze blew through the yard.

Dahlia drifted down through the branch and sank slowly to the ground.

The twins were still busy in the flowerbeds; only their feet and ankles could be seen protruding from the dark soil.

Various uprooted plants were scattered all around them. Junie's foot shot out and connected with a tall sunflower, slicing it neatly off at the stem. As Dahlia watched, the perfect expired flower pulled away from the dying plant and rose slowly into the air. It made her smile, remembering another sunflower all those days ago—and how much her life had changed since then! This would make a lovely addition to a ghost garden, she thought to herself. But she didn't move to grab it, just watched as it drifted up into the sky until it was out of sight.

Then she slipped through the outer wall into Silverton Manor, feeling empty and more than a little bit lost.

Inside, Mrs. Day was moving around a kitchen overflowing with half-filled bowls, cookbooks, and open cartons and containers. A roaring oven pumped waves of healthy, orange-red heat into the cheery room. Poppy sat on a high stool, a notebook in hand, half-scribbling and half-singing to herself.

One floor up, Mr. Day crouched behind a freshly painted desert scene, holding up two Arabian-looking puppets, who were wrestling over a large fish. Dahlia smiled and kept moving. She arrived at the attic room and wisped through the door. Oliver lay on his bed, with his legs crossed. He looked like he had been waiting for something, but at this moment he was fast asleep.

Then she saw two things. On the bed next to Oliver sat the Seesaw. And next to the Seesaw, a note:

Dahlia:

Are you still around? I've got an idea for how to get the Seesaw working again. But I need your help. Maybe we could have another adventure?

Oliver

Dahlia smiled to herself. She flitted over to the desk, as a feeling started to grow inside her chest, a feeling as cozy as a down coverlet, as warm as a cup of tea, as just-right as a blazing fire in a room stuffed with friends.

With friends . . . yes.

Concentrating hard, Dahlia hooked a small pair of scissors off Oliver's desk. She zipped back and with a few quick snips, finished what she needed to do. Then she tucked her legs under her and curled up on Oliver's bed, waiting for him to wake up.

Next to his hands were two neatly snipped-out clippings from his note:

still around
adventure

Far over her head, the barrier was gone. Dahlia could go anywhere she pleased. But for right now, this minute, she was very happy to stay right where she was.

Acknowledgments

Before anything else, this story was Dahlia's. I got to know her word by word, line by line, in my then-basement office room all the way back in 2003. Her story started out very differently and, over the years, received considerable enthusiasm from readers, yet there was always the sense of not being quite *there* yet. It wasn't until more recently, when I dove back into Dahlia's world, that I realized that Oliver had his own story to tell. And bringing his tale to life was the spark that lit the whole book on fire.

Still, Dahlia's road to publication was a circuitous one, and I'm sure that more people have had a hand in shaping this book than I can accurately give remembrance to. To each of you here listed, and to those whose names I've unwittingly left off: my love, thanks, and a plate of endlessly replicating virtual brownies.

First and foremost, Erin Murphy, who was intrigued by

Dahlia's almost-story way back when she first signed me on as a fledgling author. Next, Stacy Cantor Abrams, who first fell in love with Dahlia and her crew, and then Mary Kate Castellani, who took over so capably in the manuscript's care and feeding. Of course and always, Kim and Lauren and Zack, who have been part of the process since the beginning.

And to the many others who have had a hand in critiquing, guiding, shaping, idea-brainstorming, and otherwise helping make this story what it is, I couldn't have done it without you: Kristin Kladstrup, Kate Messner, Debbie Kovacs, Kip Wilson, Julie Phillipps, Natalie Lorenzi, and the fabulous Newton Group critiquers.

Lastly, but far from leastly: to Marietta Zacker I dedicate all the periods in this book, and to Princess Elena Mechlin, all the semicolons. Use them wisely. And on the title, ladies—you totally called it.